I0649508

Blinded By Love

By: Chyna S.

Blinded by Love is a work of fiction. Names, characters, places and incidents are the product of the author's imagination or are fictitious. Any resemblance to actual events, locales, or persons, living or dead, is entirely coincidental.

Copyright ©2014 Chyna S.

All rights reserved

No part of this book may be reproduced without the consent of the publisher, except brief quotes used in review only.

ISBN-13:978-0692489680

ISBN-10:0692489681

Library of Congress Control Number: 2015946527

Manufactured in the United States of America

This book is dedicated to:

My relative, Michael Wandick, who lost his life to domestic violence,

And to my God-sister, Michelle Boykins, who lost her life to domestic violence.

To *Every Woman*, who has been or is in a 'Blinded by Love' relationship / marriage etc. Keep your head up and Love you first.

End Domestic Violence!

Intro

A touching story that many women have been through; have you ever been 'Blinded by Love?' Have you ever been or are being lied to, cheated on, walked over, used, and abused? Were you or are you so tired of it and you don't know what to do? Being 'Blinded by Love', can break your heart, have your mind gone, and doing things that you know is not right, however, you are still doing them, due to the fact that you are 'Blinded by Love'. Being in a 'Blinded by Love' situation can be a detriment to one's health and can lead to someone being hurt, mentally or physically.

Are you…?

Ignoring reality, not seeing the wrong he is doing.

Like being addicted to a drug and just can't and don't want to let go.

Do the bad outweigh the good?

Don't be hooked on a dream, as you will be a fool. You don't want to have low confidence; high confidence is what you should have. Being 'Blinded by Love' can lead one to have low self-esteem, with a wall always up.

You see the negative bad things; however, you are ignoring the signs because you *Love* this person so much and you want this person to *Love* you back. Open your eyes and stop being *blinded* by false actions.

Deep down inside, you know that you are not happy, but you still choose to stay. You are the first priority; make sure that you are happy before trying and making your mate happy, especially one that's not even worried about you being happy.

Stop being in denial and leave before it is too late…

Chapter 1

Brooklyn's world turned upside down the day she found out she was pregnant. For her it was bittersweet; she was full of emotions, and stressed out at times, she felt as if she was in this cold world alone. She found herself always digging herself out when she was in a hole. She always wondered why life kept pushing her into a corner; no matter how hard she tried, things always seemed to go left. They say you are not supposed to question, however, that was hard for her to do; especially knowing she was a good person, and bad continued to come her way.

She knew she wasn't the only one going through things; *"But, damn, come on now. Why me?"* she constantly asked. She found herself asking, *"Where did I go wrong? Is my faith continuing to be tested? If so, why? I never gave up on you."* Referring to God, Brooklyn had always kept her faith and stood on her own two feet. Nevertheless, still she wondered, *"Damn, why me?"* She held all her hurt and pain inside, covering it up with a smile as if nothing was wrong. While all the time, her feet were hurting and sore from walking long miles and going through so much abuse and pain. She tried so hard to keep going,

1

make it to the top, and succeed trying not to give up. She continued to pray, on her knees, praying for all her hurt, pain, and struggles to go away.

Brooklyn had been in and out of foster homes rarely shown love. Their mother Bridgette, and their mother's boyfriend who went by the name, J-Mack, physically and mentally abused her and her eldest sister Brittney. Brooklyn had a golden dark skin complexion, chubby cheeks, and a head full of hair. She was more of the quiet type, very observant, nice and always thinking. At seventeen, she met and fell in love with Terrence, Terrence Carter, her child's father. At the time, he was eighteen years old. He was all she knew and all she had. She had been with him for eleven years. He had her going through so many emotional vicissitudes after her being with him for so long.

In the beginning, Terrence *was the one*. He was there for her; he took care of her, loved her, and treated her better than anybody she had ever been with— including family. He took care of everything, anything Brooklyn wanted or needed; he made it happen. She didn't have to want for anything; she had it made. Although she worked and had her own income, she didn't have to spend on anything. All she paid were her credit card bills. She had a shoe fetish, so her money went on nice fancy shoes. One thing she did for sure was made sure she had a secret bank account that only she knew about, keeping a stash just in case a rainy day came her way… The money Terrence was giving her; she would take it and put it in her secret account. He had money; he wasn't tripping off what she was doing with it.

After his mother died, he collected her insurance benefits; he was her beneficiary. After being secretly abused by her husband his father, she switched beneficiaries without anyone knowing. She didn't die from his abuse, she died because her husband mistress chased and ran her off the 91 freeway, heading towards Bellflower. Terrence came into two hundred thousand dollars. He got his business license and invested some of the money in a Coin Laundry located in Gardena. His business ran good and made a decent amount of money. He then got caught up in the drug game.

***

Brittney had a tan neutral skin tone, not so quiet, and wasn't as nice as Brooklyn. Her mother, Bridgette was a natural beauty; she stood mid-height, soft brown skin, and shoulder-length hair, very attractive— that's until she met James.

Before Bridgette met James, known as J-Mack, she had it going on; she worked as a Paralegal for Benjamin & Steller's Law Firm. She was bringing in good money for her and her girls…

"Hi, how can I help you?" Bridgette asked the man that approached her as she was sitting at the front desk at the law firm.

"Yes, I have an appointment with, Steller," James responded. *"Damn, she looks good,"* he then thought.

Once their eyes connected, Bridgette thought to herself, *"Nope, can't mess with the clients."* She never liked mixing business with pleasure. She immediately came out of lalaland. "Okay and sign here, thank you," she said, referring to the sign in sheet. "You can have a seat in the waiting area over there."

He sat down in one of the plush chairs in the waiting room, grabbed a magazine off the stand near his seat, and crossed his legs.

"Mm, James Mack." she said as she picked up the sign in sheet to see his name.

James was an aggressive, tall, mean looking person. However, Bridgette didn't see that; she saw an attractive sexy man. Knowing his criminal background, she looked past that, always feeling that a person has room to change. He served time in the pen for robbery and attempted murder. It was something about him that Bridgette liked. Some women like the aggressive look, and she was one of them.

3

For some reason, she wanted to show him what she was working with. Usually, she would just call the client's name and point them in the direction they needed to go. This time, she got up and walked over to the waiting area where he was sitting.

She was wearing a form-fitting black and white business pinstripe pantsuit; her back side filled it out nicely, with the shape she had, it was hard for her to hide it. "Mr. Mack, Steller is ready for you now."

He got up and followed her lead, staring directly at her ass. You could only imagine the thought that ran through his head.

After having his appointment with the Lawyer, he stopped Bridgette, as she sped walked down the hallway. "Excuse me; you never gave me your name."

"And you never asked, either."

"Oh, you feisty, huh?"

"Excuse me,"

"Just how I like 'em," James said, looking her up and down, "You got a man?"

"Why is it your concern?" she said playing hard to get.

"I guess that's a no,"

"Well, you have a good day, Mr. Mack."

"Yeah, alright, I'll be seeing you soon, sexy." he told her and then walked off.

"He got his nerves," she said to herself before running to answer the phone. "Benjamin and Steller's Law Firm how can I help you?"…

After several tries and visits to the Firm, James was finally able to win Bridgette over. In the beginning, as most relationships, theirs was great. They fell in love, so they thought.

She didn't see anything wrong with his past, hell she had a past herself, who was she to judge. They would share everything with each other. Well, he was giving her bits and pieces of his life, while she was open and honest about hers. Well, she wasn't quite honest either, because she never told him that she had and is still having an affair with her boss, Mr. Benjamin himself. Their relationship began to get rocky and things began to spiral left.

After James told her that his hustling and drug days were over, she came to find out it was all a lie and how much money he had stolen from her, she just couldn't believe. That wasn't just it, not just one or two, but over three times she caught him cheating, and along with all that, she found out he was pimping. She still stayed with him no matter what. She felt she wasn't letting what she build break. To her, she was standing by her man. From how he was, mistreating and disrespecting her, her way of coping turned to her dipping her nose in powder, which led to bigger drugs. Not being thrown off her game, she continued to work, just slacking a bit here and there. She was head over heels for him despite he was no good. Focused and blinded over him she hardly had time for Brittney and Brooklyn. J-Mack never once tried to stop her from using; he just continued to feed her what she fiend for…

The girls never knew what she saw in him. He had Bridgette brainwashed and gone off the drugs. Bridgette would sit on the end of her king size bed giving herself that good ol' dose of 'Magic'… As the flowing rush goes through those veins of hers, once those eyes rolled up and she got to leaning and nodding, J-Mack would creep his perverted self in Brittney and Brooklyn's rooms one at a time, molesting each of them. They both were scared and were told not to tell, because if they tell the Department of Children and Family Services would come and separate the two of them and they will not see each other or their mother ever again. *He was a monster.* That went on for a good three years. It started when they were around six and seven years old.

***

One late night, Brittney woke up out her sleep in need of using the bathroom. She would wet herself a lot due to all the sexual abuse she was enduring. This night she woke up on time and headed for the bathroom. As she walked past Brooklyn's room, she heard her crying, sobbing. She was already aware of the abuse her sister was going through because it was happening to her too. Something came through her and, this time, she walked in Brooklyn's room when she saw that J-Mack wasn't around she consoled her sister, holding her tight.

"He's coming back," Brooklyn cried, whispering to her sister.

"Ok, it's going to be alright, sister, just wait for it," Brittney responded. She went to go hide in the closet slowly, quietly closing the door, leaving it cracked just enough for her to see through. She stood there and watched... He walked in silently closed the door and locked it behind him. Her eyes were so big she didn't know what to do; she began to tremble but remained quiet.

Brooklyn didn't know what she meant by saying, 'Wait for it.' *"Wait for it, wait for what?"* she thought scared. *"Is she out of her mind?"*

J-Mack walked in, "Didn't I tell you to stop all that damn crying and have those tears wiped up by the time I got back?" he told her in a harsh tone as he sat beside her on the bed rubbing her leg slowly sliding his hand up her light blue gown.

She laid on her side and balled up into a fetal position, trembling, rocking herself back and forth. At this time, Brooklyn was nine and Brittney was ten. They were just one year apart and close as ever, you would have thought they were twins; they looked a lot alike. They were so close that, if one got in trouble the other would get herself in trouble too or they would take each other's whippings.

The further J-Mack put his hand up her gown, the harder she would weep. *"Sister, please, help me."* she cried repeating in her head.

"Get your dirty, filthy ass hands off of my little sister, right now!" Brittney came out the closet, stood behind him and demanded in a heartbroken but stern tone.

He paused and turned around with a smirk on his gritty looking face, "You little…"

Brittney had a .380 Smith & Wesson pointed right at his forehead. "No more," she stated, gun already cocked and ready.

Earlier that day, Brittney knew that Bridgette and J-Mack were high and loaded, they had already talked about staying in the house and just lounge around; they all knew what that meant– get high all day. When J-Mack nodded and fell asleep, Brittney snuck in their room grabbed his .380 he had in his shoebox, ran into the bathroom, checked to make sure it was loaded and ready; and it was, she knew she was taking a chance, however, she didn't care; she ran to her room and hid it, and now ready to use it…

Stunned and shocked, "How in the hell you get my gun?" he asked her nervously.

"Brooklyn, come over here," she was scared to move. "Brooklyn, it's okay, come on now, trust me." Brooklyn jumped up as quickly as she could, ran, and stood behind her sister but closer to the closet. "Don't worry about how I got your gun, worry about this being the last time you will ever put your hands on us again."

"If you don't give me my…" he said, reaching for the gun. Boom! Boom! Brittney squeezed two shots square dead in his head. They were both shocked, no words came out, but their mouths hung open. Bridgette continued to sleep through the sound of the gun going off. Brittney stood over his lifeless body just looking down at it, feeling no pain whatsoever. She was just glad that he wouldn't be around anymore. She saved her sister, her mother, and her own life.

Brooklyn ran to her sister hugging her as tight as she can. "What are we gonna do now?" she asked softly.

"Pray and stick together."

Everything happened so quickly...

The girls thought that they would be in some kind of trouble after what escalated. Therefore, they bent the truth, *just a little bit.* They knew Social Services were going to get them, they just hoped for the best, to stay together no matter what. No charges were brought against the girls. From the story they told, it was pure self-defense. Moreover, from all the medical exams they both had, showed that they were abused, mentally and physically— so, they were taken from their mother. Bridgette had to take parenting classes and was sent to a sober living to get herself together.

At a time before, the girls tried to tell their mother about what J-Mack was doing to them, but she didn't believe them; she shined them on, told them to get their lying asses out of her face, and moved on like nothing was ever said. They felt some type of way about that and will never forget it. That day they knew she chose him over them. Therefore, when they were taken away from her, they were relieved; she was not a good parent to them; however, they were glad for her when they found out that she was going to a program to get better.

Bridgette was sick, her girls were gone and J-Mack was dead. All she had left of him were bittersweet memories. While going through rehab, she continued to go to work. It took a lot out of her to get up and do what she needed to do.

She finished her 30-day program and continued with her normal life. She tried a few times to get Brooklyn and Brittney back, however, things just weren't going in her favor. She had failed one too many drug tests. Life had become hard for her; she had no one, her girls didn't even want to be with her anymore.

She failed them, big time. They resented her, she didn't protect them. *Where was she when they needed her the most?* She was in a zone, lalaland, somewhere in the clouds. J-Mack had changed her. Bridgette left the heroin alone after his death, she never liked how it made her feel anyway; how it would have her out and always down. To keep afloat, she continued dipping in cocaine; it kept her focused and ready to face her life challenges. To her, it was her medication; she didn't look at it as a drug.

She never gave up trying to get her girls back. But she did take a break. Maybe they will come to her, she would think. She explained her situation to her boss and he accepted it with deep compassion and sympathy. Her drug habit was her secret, no one needed to know that. Benjamin would give her money each month to give to Brittney and Brooklyn. She would find out where they were placed and made sure she gave them five hundred dollars each a month; they never turned it down, but still didn't want to see her. That alone gave Bridgette hope that they would one day accept her back and talk to her again. Bridgette beat herself up every day that she wasn't there for them. How could she have let James, that monster around or near them? The thought of what he had done to them hunted her. Brooklyn and Brittney didn't know if they wanted to forgive her or not. Their dad already failed them by leaving before they were born, and never looked back. Their life growing up wasn't easy.

Growing up in the system was very much hard for Brooklyn and Brittney. They both got into many fights with different females they were living with. No matter what happened, they always stayed together they were never split apart. One social worker gave them her word that she would do her best to keep them together. Clothing and other personal items would always come up missing, causing problems within the house amongst the girls. With a house full of females, they were bound to clash…

Brittney and Brooklyn knew if they tried to leave, they would not make it out in the streets on their own. Therefore, they rode it out until they hit eighteen…

Chapter 2

"Hey, Brittney, have you seen my toothpaste?"

"No, it's not in your drawer?"

"No, it's gone,"

"Really, I have an extra one,"

"Thanks, but that's not the point, though. Somebody stole my shit."

They hated being in that foster home. Nothing was ever done when their things came up missing. Being in the foster home, the two girls tried to stay out of trouble as much as they could. However, with their personal things coming up missing and the nit-picking, was hard for them to do.

Brooklyn walked off into another room in the house. "Tanisha, did you take my toothpaste?" she was the first person she asked because she was caught stealing something of Brittney's before.

"No. Why would I take your toothpaste, and I have my own?"

"Mm," Brooklyn said, irritated. She looked Tanisha up and down, "Y'all bitches are gone get enough of touching my shit!"

"Girl, ain't nobody touched your shit!" Latoya blurted out. She was another foster child that stayed in the home.

At this time, Brittney walked in the room. "If y'all got my sister's shit just give it to her,"

"Nobody has her shit," Tanisha responded, pulling her hair in a ponytail.

"Okay, well, I'll just do a sweep myself then," Brooklyn told them approaching one of their dressers to look through them.

"Uh, uh, you not 'bout to go through my stuff; I said, I don't have your toothpaste," Tanisha told her stepping in front of her.

"You must be feeling guilty," Brittney told Tanisha.

"You can get out my face, and move out my way!" Brooklyn said to Tanisha. She reached around her to pull open the drawer. When Tanisha pushed her hand away, Brooklyn hit her with two punches to the face, and then stepped back with her guards up. "What's up, bitch!"

They squared off going toe-to-toe for a minute. Latoya and Brittney stood watching for a minute and then tried to break them up.

"Come on, Brook, before Mrs. Harris, come in here." Mrs. Harris was their foster mother. She raised them from the time they were put in the system. She continued trying to pull and loosen their grip on each other.

"Let them fight!" Latoya said.

"You would say that, bitch!"

They started back swinging on each other falling to the floor with Brooklyn on top of Tanisha. Latoya started pulling Brooklyn off Tanisha. Before she could get her all the way off her, Tanisha kicked Brooklyn in the face. She felt the kick, but having so much anger and rage in her, it didn't faze her.

Tanisha got up off the ground. "Ah, look at your face, bitch!" she said, breathing heavy and fast, but smiling.

They were both trying to catch their breath. Brittney looked over at her sister's face and flipped out; she had a small open cut under her eye. Brittney took off on Tanisha knocking her on the bed; she jumped on top of her and started drilling her. Latoya jumped in and started hitting Brittney in the back of the head trying to get her off Tanisha. As soon as Brooklyn was about to get on Latoya, Mrs. Harris and Troy, another foster child that stayed in the home heard all the commotion and ran in there to break the girls up.

"What in the Sam's hell are yall in here doing? Are y'all out of your minds?" After breaking them up and gaining some control of the situation, the girls stood around talking mess to each other, breathing hard with their hair everywhere. "Look at y'all looking like some damn heathens!"

"One of them stole my toothpaste out of my drawer,"

"Well, you should have brought your ass to me and said something,"

"The last time I told you me and my sister's stuff was missing, you said you would replace it, and you never did. So, what I look like telling you again, if you didn't do nothing the other times."

"You can take your smart ass mouth in your room,"

"I hate it here! I can't wait to get the fuck out of this damn hellhole!"

"Brooklyn, just go in the room," Troy told her.

"And, you shut your gay ass up, bitch!" she told him.

"Take your disrespectful ass out of here, as a matter of fact go outside, and cool off!" Mrs. Harris told her.

Brittney and Brooklyn went in their room, fixed themselves up, and went for a walk.

They really hated living in that house; it was as if they were living in *'The Bad Girls Club'*. Constant fights, stealing, favoritism, childishness, the list goes on... What didn't happen in that house?

There was a time before when Brooklyn walked in on Troy and Ebony having sex. Ebony lived in the house too. Mrs. Harris turned her in for running away too many times and her uncontrollable behavior. She was a hothead; she was wild and diagnosed with, bipolar. She had her first abortion when she was twelve years old, then her second one at fourteen and soon after a miscarriage. She got so angry one day, hauled off and hit Mrs. Harris; that is what drew the line for her. Troy also had a few issues, an identity crisis. He was once caught dressing up in Brittney's clothes. The problems never ended.

***

"Ugh, I can't wait to get out of that damn house, ugh!" Brooklyn cried to her big sister.

Brittney put an arm around her shoulder, "We'll be out of there soon."

"Yeah, I know."

"Hey, Brittney, where you headed to?" Vince asked as he pulled alongside the curb, as they strolled down the street. Vince was an older guy that always hit on Brittney every time he would see her. He stayed around their neighborhood.

She waved, "Hey, Vince. Just taking a walk to the store,"

"You almost ready for me?" he asked her.

"No, not yet," she said shyly. He knew she was underage; he was waiting until she turned eighteen. Older men would always hit on her. Actually, she had thoughts of only dating older men. She always said that younger guys or guys her age were immature and childish and was only out for one thing, the goodies.

"Girl, his old ass still trying to get with you," Brooklyn said giggling.

"I know, right."

"Alright, I'll be waiting," he responded thirstily driving off.

"He on you, girl. He gone be jumping out the bushes like, 'Bri, is you ready for me,'" they both laughed.

"Forget you," she said, shoving her lightly.

They continued walking to the store, got them some junk food, and stood around for a minute talking to a few guys from their neighborhood. Bored with their conversations and seeing all they were trying to do was get in their pants, they headed back home, a place they dreaded to go back to.

***

Boom! Two masked men kicked open Bridgette's front door with their guns drawn. One holding a 9mm Luger in one hand, and a .45 Caliber in the other, the other man had drawn a Hi-Point Carbine .45. Immediately, Brittney and Brooklyn jumped off the couch from watching TV, screamed, and jetted towards their room. When Bridgette ran out her room, one of the men grabbed her by her hair and threw her to the floor.

"¿Dónde está la droga y el dinero, perra?" one man told her.

"What, I don't have nothing. What do you want?" Bridgette cried.

"Where the dope and money at, bitch?" the other man told her, and then ran looking for the girls.

"I don't have any money and dope! Please, let me go!" she cried.

By the time the other man made it to the girls, they were both under Brittney's bed, crying.

The girls had been through and seen a lot throughout their lives. After being tied up for so long, Bridgette told the men where the money and drugs were. After they got what they were looking for, they untied her and left, leaving them unharmed.

"Brooklyn, Brittney!" Bridgette yelled, running through the hallway.

"Momma!" Bridgette hollered. "Come on, Brooklyn." She grabbed her hand and ran towards their mother.

"Oh my God, are you guys ok?"

They were both scared, crying as their mother held them in her arms. Hysterically, she grabbed her phone and called, J-Mack. "We just got robbed!" she said into the receiver.

"You what, bitch, what the fuck you just say?"

"Bitch, I'm telling you we just been robbed, and the first thing you do is call me a bitch!"

"I'm on my way." he told her, and then hung up in her face.

Chyna S.

After getting beat up one night by J-Mack, Bridgette was hurt and pissed, she knew she couldn't beat him up, she wanted revenge; she had her own house set up to be robbed. She waited a couple of weeks until things cooled down between them and came up with a plan that she knew would hurt him. Cheating wouldn't have hurt him; he wouldn't have believed her anyway. But she knew coming up short on funds and goods would really hurt him.

Chapter 3

"Hey, Brooklyn, hold up for a sec!" Terrence yelled skipping behind her as she walked out the school gate heading home.

She turned around, "Hey, what's up, Terrence?"

"I just wanted to holla' at you for a second; what's up with you?"

"Nothing; why what's up?"

Terrence was one of the popular guys at school; he was a player that played many girls. The females loved him. His light brown skin, hazel eyes, and for an eighteen-year-old he had a body.

"I been checking you out and want to get to know you a little better. What you say you shoot me your number and let me take you out this weekend?"

"Mm... I don't know," she responded hesitantly, turning up her face. "Wait a minute, don't you go with... what's her name... Monica," she said out as if she was guessing an answer on family feud.

"Nah, well, we used to fuck around, but not no more,"

"Oh, is that right. Oh, okay, well..." as she got ready to give him her number, she said, "and, don't be trying to play no games."

"Girl, what you mean, don't be trying to play games? You good, don't trip."

Feeling that he had no reason to lie, Brooklyn went on and gave him her number. "Alright, I'ma hit you up a little later," he told her.

"Alright,"

"I know you did not just give that dude your number?" Brittney said as she walked up.

"Yeah, girl, why you say that?" Brooklyn asked eager to know.

"Girl, he is a player, and he mess with that one skanky trick... what's her name..."

"Monica, well, he said they're not together."

"Is that right? Believe it if you want to."

Brittney left Brooklyn in thought thinking was Terrence really telling the truth? She hoped that he was telling the truth, *"Why would he lie, there was no need."* She always liked Terrence; however, she kept that to herself. That's why it wasn't much hesitation before giving him her number.

Brittney was her 'Sister's Keeper', always keeping a close eye on her making sure she was protected and safe, especially when a male figure was present.

***

A good six months into her and Terrence's relationship, Brooklyn ran into a situation about, Terrence…

Brooklyn walked up the stairs into her Aunt Bailey's house. Before she could get in and get comfortable, "Brooklyn, let me talk to you for a minute," Monica said getting up from the couch.

"How does this bitch know my auntie?" Brooklyn asked herself. *"Damn, it's a small world."*

Brooklyn hadn't been to her aunt's house in a while, but whenever she was over there, she never ran into Monica. She never even heard her name being spoken of either, so that was a shocker to her.

"Damn…" Brooklyn responded ignoring Monica. "Hey, Auntie Bailey, how are you doing?" She reached in giving her a hug.

"I'm good, baby. Oh, you two know each other?" Aunt Bailey asked, pointing from one girl to another, clueless as to what was going on.

Both girls looked at each other with an attitude. "Yeah, we do, Bailey," Monica answered.

Brooklyn turned to Monica, "What's up?"

"So, what's up with you and Terrence? I'm hearing that you fucking him,"

"Nah, I'm not fucking him yet. However, I have been dating him. He said y'all weren't together anymore anyway." she responded nonchalantly.

"He is a damn lie; don't believe everything you hear and everything his lying ass say."

"Okay, well, that's your opinion…"

One of Terrence cousins lived in the same building as Bailey, so Terrence was always over there kicking it with Brooklyn. She thought, *"If he is still messing with her, where and when was she getting her time?"* Terrence and Brooklyn were spending a lot of time together. She tried to stay away from her foster home as much and as long as possible, so most of her time spent away was with him.

Monica stepped to Brooklyn, "Just know, that is my man and I suggest you leave him alone,"

"If you don't get yo' ass out my face, you gone regret you ever tried to step to me. And, until Terrence tells me differently, I'm not going anywhere,"

Bailey sat there looking, pulling on a cigarette lost. "Girls, girls, now, whatever is going on, I know it's not that serious and worth it. Y'all chill out,"

"It's cool, Bailey," Monica said. "I'm about to leave anyway." Monica looked Brooklyn up and down, turned around, and walked out the door.

"What the hell was all that about?" Bailey asked.

Brooklyn sat on the couch and was pissed; in that little time she had already caught feelings, and not from sex; she been withholding that. Just by what he was telling her and doing for her; everything she wanted to hear, and everything she needed, he did that. She never received that, so she yearned for it. It felt good to be told 'I love you' and 'you are beautiful', and those are some of the things he told her.

"She and Terrence used to mess around. I'm with him now, so I guess she got a problem with it," she told her.

"Oh, is that right? I guess that's why she used to always be downstairs."

"Maybe,"

"Well, honey, you make sure you keep your eyes and your mind open and don't let that heart get out too quickly. These boys can be trouble before you know it."

"I know, Auntie."

***

She didn't call him; she waited until he showed up. "Let me talk to you for a second, Terrence," Brooklyn said as she came into his cousin, Anthony's house waving her hand with an attitude.

"Hold on for a sec, I'll be out there." Brooklyn rolled her eyes, turned around and walked outside. Terrence sat there until he was finished rolling his blunt.

"Hi, Brook," one of the little kids said as they walked by, grabbed a jump rope off the ground and began jumping.

Brooklyn stood there with her arms folded with attitude and sass. She hadn't even been with him a good six months, and it was already problems.

"What's up, what you got to talk to me about?" Terrence asked when he walked out the door.

"What's going on with you and Monica? I just had a talk with her over at my Aunt Bailey's house. She said y'all still together. What's up with that?"

"That's why you walking around here with that look on yo' face? Now if you believe some shit like that, you crazy. First of all, a majority of my time is spent with you. That girl is crazy as hell, she wish we were still together."

"We have been spending a lot of time together," she thought. *"But, that don't really mean nothing, plus we don't spend nights together, so he could be giving her that time at night."*

"So, you gone believe that bullshit?" he asked, taking her out her thoughts.

"Hmm…" she said with a twisted lip, "you bet not be playing with my heart and emotions, I take that very seriously,"

"Girl," he said, grabbing her in close, hugging her, "you need to chill out; I'm not playing with your heart and emotions."

"You bet not be," she looked up and kissed him, then bit down on her bottom lip seductively.

"I don't know why you playing, you need to stop holding back." he said as he stepped back to check her out.

Brooklyn, grew up to be a beauty and at the age of 17 had a body of a 25-year-old.

"Don't you want to go get your hair done and hit the nail shop?" he asked her, pulling money out his wallet.

"Oh, sure," she responded, reaching to take the money. "Thanks, I'll call you later." She gave him a hug and a kiss before turning to leave.

"Oh, I see that put a smile on your face."

"Shut up, boy," she said, fanning a hand. All it took was money and material things to keep her mouth shut.

Chapter 4

Brooklyn devoted much of her time to Terrence, at times putting her sister on the back burner…

This one night, Brooklyn couldn't sleep. She sat up at home all night, and Terrence never came home. *"What?"* A No-show, she was livid. *How dare he? The nerves!* She sat in her pitch-dark living room in complete silence, thinking. Thinking about where he could have been. After calling his phone so many times that night, he eventually turned his phone off; she was going straight to voice mail… *"That mutha' fucka',"*

Daylight broke, the light shined through her blinds as she lay in bed with a leg slightly hanging from under the cover. When she turned over to look at the digital clock radio, it read 6:12 a.m. His side was still cold because he never came home.

"Fucking asshole," She was over pissed she was heated. *"This man still not home,"* she thought to herself as she sat up in her bed. She grabbed her phone off the nightstand; there were no missed calls or any text from him so she tried his number again; nothing… It went straight to voice mail.

She called Anthony. "Hey, Anthony, have you heard from, Terrence?" Brooklyn knew it was too early in the morning to be calling around looking for a man, a man that should have been at home in bed with her, but she didn't care. Furthermore, Anthony was like a brother to her.

"Nah, I haven't heard from him since he left my spot last night."

"Hmm, is that so? Okay," she responded and hung up.

Anthony looked at his phone, shook his head, turned over and went back to sleep.

The first thought that came to her mind was, he was with another woman, *a woman's first intuition.* It is rare for a man to stay the night at a guy friend's house, yes, it happens, however, she didn't think so. Time after time, she questioned what she was doing wrong. How could he not even call her at all? If she in return did the same thing, what would he have done? Whoever he was with must have been worth it.

For Terrence to have been gone late night and overnight at times; yes, this wasn't the first time– Brooklyn wondered whether he was messing with, what she had over her? To her, she was doing everything right; working, cooking, sexing him good, head game off the chain (especially when she used ice) one of her favorites, she pleased and kept him satisfied in all the right ways; so what was his point of reason for doing what he was doing and not thinking about how Brooklyn was feeling. *"Selfish bastard!"* she thought.

Terrence was Brooklyn's drug; in her mind, she needed him. He put her on a pedal stool and had her head so high nothing or nobody mattered but him. When days were spent away from him at times, she was lonely and sad. For one, she always wondered if he was cheating. For two, missing his general presence, that love that she never received growing up, that was the best feeling she had ever felt. She loved that man, so she thought. *Did he really love her back?* Was the question…?

Brooklyn was different from the rest. When she and Terrence first met, she was upfront with him, and she expected the same from him. She told him she respect an honest man, and always be up front with her, rather it hurts her or not. She felt if Terrence didn't want her anymore, he should've been a man and told her that; but it never came out his mouth. Although Terrence was an asshole at times, he would still push her to do her best. For some reason, Brooklyn thought her life would be nothing without him. He talked a good game, and she fell for it all. He was her first relationship, her first love; he is whom she gave her precious gem to for the first time.

***

This one morning, Brooklyn got out of bed wearing a LACE-TRIM HENLEY TANK and some LACE-WAIST SHORTIE PANTIES that had VICTORIA'S SECRET written all over them. She loved her some Vickie's. She reached in her sock drawer, grabbed, and slipped on her KNEE-HIGH SOCKS and her UGG boots. In the process of doing so, she heard a vibrating noise... She thought, *"I'm tripping."* Shook her head, and continued to go freshen up, make her morning coffee, and breakfast before work... She noticed the shower water running, and heard the noise again, this time following where it was coming from. She paused, stopped to listen, nothing. Then there it goes again... The noise led her to Terrence's side of the bed, to his pants he had on the floor. Inside of his pants pocket was his phone vibrating. *Somebody was blowing his phone up.* Terrence was in the bathroom in the shower. Usually, he would take his phone in there with him, but this particular time he must have had his mind on something else and forgot about it.

Brooklyn had the opportunity to answer it since it wasn't stuck to his hip. "Hello," she answered. There was a pause and then the phone hung up. The phone went off again, "Yes," Brooklyn said with an attitude.

"Hello, can I speak to, T?" the woman on the other end asked with a soft tone.

"Can you speak to, 'T'? Who's calling?"

"Dion,"

"Dion… Where he knows you from and why are you calling him at this time in the morning?" It was 7:30 a.m.

"Oh, well from my knowledge, he told me it was okay to call him anytime. Plus, I wanted to tell him, happy birthday,"

"Oh, is that right? He didn't tell you he was in a relationship?"

"Well, not really, he said it was complicated,"

"Mm, where you meet him at, how do you know him?"

"I met him around, been knowing him for a minute; we just friends."

"Friends, well, you one friend I ain't heard about. So, 'friend', are you fucking my man?"

There was a pause. "You might want to talk to 'your man'; 'cause obviously there is a lack of communication between y'all,"

Brooklyn laughed. Her question was never answered, "So, you mean to tell me, you called his phone at 7:30 in the mutha' fuckin' morning to tell him happy birthday'? Well, look it here, Ms. Dion. Terrence is in a relationship, we live together and this is nothing new. So, I would appreciate it if you respect that, and don't call his phone anymore or have any more dealings with him; and… Don't tell me you will stop when he tells you to. This is going to be your first and last warning from his woman. Whatever he tells you, is all lies, just know that." Click. Brooklyn said no more, didn't let Dion get a word in and hung up the phone.

She looked at his text messages… One message read from sender (Shawn), **"Hey, sexy, you still coming through later?"**

"What?" Brooklyn thought. *"Coming through, later?"*

"Yeah, where you want me to meet you again?" Brooklyn sent a text back as if she was, Terrence.

"Yo' crazy ass needs to stop smoking. Didn't you say you were coming to my house?"

"Yeah, yeah, got thrown off, a lot has been going on. Text me the address again,"

"Ok."

As soon as the text came through with the address, Brooklyn heard the shower water go off, grabbed a pen from the dresser, and wrote the address and phone number down, and deleted the messages.

Terrence walked in the room right after she put his phone back up, with his towel wrapped around his waist, revealing a part of his sexy 'V' cut. She acted as if she was looking for something under the bed.

"What you doing?" he asked her.

"I was looking for my, uh, uh… Oh, never mind, I just remembered where I put it," she quickly lied standing up. "Happy birthday," she told him, giving him a kiss. "What you got planned for later?"

"Me and the boys going out for some drinks and to shoot a little pool,"

"Oh, okay. Well, I have to work a double tonight, so have fun," she said turning to walk off. She was an LVN working as a Charge Nurse in a Convalescent Hospital. She was always at work, which gave Terrence more than enough alone time.

"Who in the fuck is, Dion?" she thought as she walked out the room to go to the bathroom. It was killing her inside not to say anything to him about it. She freshened up and went to the kitchen to make her coffee and breakfast. She was gone make him a birthday breakfast, but she thought, *"Let, Dion and Shawn make it."* The whole time, Brooklyn couldn't get her mind off that text message and phone call; mainly the text...

Chapter 5

Brooklyn lied to Terrence about having to work a double. When she knew he was long gone from the house, she headed back home to change her clothes. She changed into all black; she was going on a mission to the address that she received from Terrence's phone. She headed out of Sierra Gardens Apartments. It was no shame in her game; she needed to see for herself. Once it got dark, she called Brittney. "B, come ride with me somewhere real quick," she told her.

"Alright, come get me. Call me when you get outside. I don't need, Paul all in my business; you know his nosey ass," they both laughed. "Okay." they hung up the phones.

Although at times, Brooklyn would put Brittney on the back burner for Terrence, she would still jump whenever she would call. Plus, how boring her friend, Paul was, she couldn't wait to get out and get away. All he wanted to do was play rummy, watch movies, and drink beer. Paul was an older guy that she was dating that she would see from time to time.

***

"I keep telling you, you need to leave his no good ass alone," Brittney told Brooklyn as they rode to the address that she received from Terrence's text message.

Brooklyn always had her gut feeling, but never seen anything for her own eyes until she read the text message from, Shawn.

"Well, I want to see for my damn self, if that's alright with you."

"Fine, but…"

"There go a car pulling up," Brooklyn said, stopping her in mid-sentence.

"Then park right here."

Brooklyn had brought her a little bucket (a low-key car) for days like this. She never parked it in her building; she would park it down the street from her house.

She parked the car some houses down from where the car pulled up. They both sat low in their seats so they couldn't be seen. A couple of guys got out the car stood in front of the house and started conversing with one another. Another car pulled up, this time, it was, Terrence. Brooklyn sat up a little… "What is he doing?"

"Girl, you probably wrote down the wrong address,"

"Shut up, no I didn't,"

"I don't see any signs of any women,"

"We just have to wait and see."

Terrence parked his car, got out, and shook hands with the two people that were standing in front of the house.

"What the hell are they doing, having a meeting?" Brittney questioned.

"I have no idea, girl."

All three men headed into the house. Nothing looked suspicious to the two of them. *Was Brooklyn tripping, did she write down the right address?* Of course, she did if Terrence was there. Something wasn't right…

"Where is the bitch at, that's all I want to know?" Brooklyn asked.

"You sure it was a female and didn't read the text wrong?" Brittney asked curious to know.

"I read the text right. I know I'm not tripping. He did say he was going to go play pool with his boys. I guess he was telling the truth. But who is the bitch that was texting?"

More men started showing up and several females, some dressed like dancers.

"Whoa!" Brittney said after seeing the women.

"Looks like they about to have a party,"

"You want to go in there?"

"Hell yeah, I want to go to the party too. Why wasn't I invited? It's other females in there, it ain't just for men."

Brooklyn drove off and drove to the corner store to get them something to drink. She purchased a bottle of Long Island Ice Tea and two Styrofoam cups. She drove back to where they were parked, poured her and her sister a drink and waited until they thought everybody was good and comfortable in the house…

***

Everybody at the party was drunk, loud, and wilding. Cups and smoke filled the air. Every other area was a stripper dancing. Everybody looked like they were in a zone, enjoying themselves. Brooklyn scanned the party in search of Terrence, but he was nowhere in sight. Nobody looked familiar to her. *"Where his ass at?"* she thought. She spotted Anthony in the crowd dancing with some half-naked stripper.

She walked up to him. "Hey, Anthony, where is, Terrence? He told me to meet him here."

Anthony looked screw faced, "Oh, he did..." he answered as to why Terrence would tell her to meet him there. Oh well, he was drunk and in la-la land with a stripper, he didn't care what was going on. "I think he walked in the back somewhere!" he yelled pointing a finger.

"Okay, thanks!" she said and walked off.

Brittney stood there looking at all the drunks' wilding out. One person was sleeping in the corner with his drink tilted in his hand while some took pictures of him laughing. *"They are on,"* she said to herself.

"Hey, B, I'ma go to the back for a second."

"Okay, here I come."

Brooklyn walked to the back and Brittney followed behind. As she walked, she still saw no sign of, Terrence. "Let me use the bathroom real quick," she said.

"Okay."

"Y'all ladies want a drink?" a man asked them as he walked by.

"No thank you, we cool," Brooklyn responded.

They walked to the bathroom and Brooklyn knocked on the door. "Just a minute." a woman's voice answered.

As the door cracked, Brooklyn looked only to see Terrence's face! "What the fuck!" Brooklyn bellowed. Her immediate reaction was to push the door open. Terrence quickly slammed the door closed. "Open this mutha' fuckin' door!" she yelled beating on the door, now kicking it. Some of the party stood around looking while other's continued partying as if nothing was going on. Brittney was so shocked, she didn't know what to do or say. "So you just gone stay yo ass in there and not come out! Alright!"

"Who in the hell is that out there?" the stripper in the bathroom asked nervously.

"My girl, that's who,"

"What? You better go out there, I'm not about to sit in this damn bathroom, I got money to make."

"Bitch, wait a minute!" he grumbled.

"Come on, Brook, let's get out of here," Brittney said feeling bad for her sister. The look on her face showed nothing but hurt and pain.

Brooklyn tried to hold herself together as if she wasn't hurt, holding in the tears that tried to run down her face. From the looks of it, Terrence wasn't coming out anytime soon. "Hell no, I'm not going anywhere."

"Come on," Brittney grabbed Brooklyn and headed to the car.

"I can't believe his punk ass. I'm so done with him. A fucking stripper, really! He was that damn desperate,"

"You need to leave his ass alone. He is no good for you, sis." Brittney told her with deep sympathy. "You deserve much better than this."

"I can't believe this shit; no, I'm going back in there."

"Brook, no!"

She snatched away and headed back in and towards the bathroom, meeting Terrence and the stripper in the hallway. "Oh, really," she said, looking from him to her.

"It's not what you think, Broo..." She slapped him as hard as she could in the face.

"Bitch!" his reflexes backhanded her and her reflexes socked the stripper.

"Now, I'm ready to go," she told Brittney. The stripper stood there holding her hand to her jaw.

"What's up man, what's going on?" Anthony asked Terrence.

"Brooklyn's ass came up in here tripping. How in the hell she knew I was here?" He was shocked and curious to know how she had known. "She told me she had to work. Damn, I fucked up."

"You alright, you good?" he asked Terrence, and then turned to the stripper, "You good, Ma?"

"Yeah, I am. Crazy bitch," she responded, looked at Terrence rolled her eyes, and then walked off.

"Brooklyn left out of here looking pissed off, what the hell you do?" Anthony asked.

"She saw me coming out the bathroom with, Shawn,"

"Shawn?"

"The stripper, man,"

"Oh, yeah, didn't know you knew her damn name."

"Man, shut yo' drunk ass up," Terrence responded playfully pushing Anthony.

***

"I'll stay at your house with you tonight," Brittney told Brooklyn as they rode to Bellflower.

"Okay, that's cool,"

"You, ok?"

"Yeah, I'm ok. I just can't believe his scandalous ass."

The rest of the way they rode in silence and Brooklyn was in deep thought.

Brittney and Brooklyn was a little different when it came to men. Brittney did more dating than jumping into relationships. After going through what she went through as a child, she didn't trust men and would only let them get so close. Brooklyn on the other hand, took to men, wanting to be in a relationship. She thought it was better to keep one man than be dating different men.

"How dare he?" she thought. *"I have given him all of me."* At times, she felt gone, but when around others a person could never tell unless it was her sister.

***

Back at the party, Terrence, Anthony, and a few other guys stood out front talking. A royal blue Acura pulled up with tinted windows. "Aye, I'll be back, I'ma leave my car parked here."

"Nigga, where you 'bout to go?" one of the guys asked.

"I'm 'bout to make a run real quick." he responded before going to get in the car.

"What's wrong with that nigga?" a guy asked.

"His girl caught him coming out the bathroom with one of the strippers,"

"Word,"

"Yeah, I saw some commotion, but I didn't know that was that dude. I thought it was some females," someone else said.

"Well, I'm about to get out of here," Anthony said and left.

***

While at the house, Brooklyn had Brittney to help her pack up Terrence's things. She wanted him out the house...

"What if he doesn't leave?" Brittney asked.

"No, he gone leave,"

"Ain't his name on the lease too?"

"Yeah, it is. Oh, well, he still has to go."

After packing all his things, they finally fell asleep. At around 3:00 a.m. Terrence came in the house, went into the room, slid off his clothes, and crept into the bed trying not to wake Brooklyn.

***

That next early morning, Brooklyn dropped Brittney off at home. When she returned, Terrence was still in the bed asleep. She went into the kitchen, grabbed the biggest bowl that she could find and filled it with cold water. She snatched the covers off him, "Get your ass up!" she said as she poured the whole bowl of water on him, wetting the bed and all.

He immediately jumped up. "What the fuck are you doing? Are you fucking crazy?"

"Get the fuck out of here. How dare you be in a bathroom with a stripper doing Lord knows what and bring your trifling ass in here in my bed and don't get in the shower!"

"You can't put me out! This ain't just yo' shit,"

"So what, you not about to be in here doing what you want to do,"

"Girl, you betta' gone somewhere with all that bullshit, I'm not going no damn where." he went to his drawer to grab him some clothes to put on. When he opened the drawer, nothing was inside. "Where my clothes at?" he looked in another drawer, nothing. "Where all my shit at?" she just stood there looking with her hands folded, mouth pushed out and twisted. He walked to the closet to see the same thing, nothing. *"This bitch packed all my shit!"* he said to himself. He walked out to the living room and saw all his things packed in some big black trash bags piled up on each other in a corner. *"This bitch tripping,"* He walked back in the room; Brooklyn was getting her some work clothes out the closet. He snatched her clothes out her hand and threw them on the floor. "If you don't unpack my shit…"

"If I don't unpack your shit, what? You think this is a joke, huh?" she walked off and started grabbing bags setting them outside on the side of the door.

He ran behind her, "What the fuck is yo' stupid ass doing?"

She looked back at him, "If I'm not mistaken, weren't you just in the bathroom with a fucking stripper?" She continued to put the bags outside.

"Get yo'…" He snatched her by the back of her head, threw her in the house, and she stumbled over a bag of clothes.

"Don't put your hands on me," she said pushing him. He started grabbing bags, putting them back in the house. The more she tried to stop him the more aggressive he became. After so long he grew tired of her trying to grab and stop him from bringing his bags in. "You not about to be disrespecting me!" she said crying.

Terrence looked through a bag and put on the first shirt that he saw. As soon as he put the shirt on, Brooklyn grabbed the back of it, pulling him away from the bag. She grabbed that same bag and headed for the door. Before she got to the door, Terrence struck her sending her to the floor. She grabbed her face crying.

"I told your ass to leave me alone!" he told her, grabbing his bag. "See what you made me do?"

She knew from that strike, he wasn't playing, so she kind of backed off. She got up off the floor. "I don't know why you bringing that shit back in here," she told him.

"Don't you have to go to work? Take your ass to work. As long as my name on this lease, I'm not going no damn where!"

Brooklyn ignored him, not saying anything. At that point, she couldn't stand him, but still loved him. She couldn't understand her feelings for him. She knew he wasn't right, however, continued to put up with all his bull. She looked at the clock on the wall, it was going on 8:30, and she had to be at work at seven that morning. *"Damn,"* she said once she realized that she was already late for work. She grabbed her phone and called her job to let them know that she was running late and would be there in a minute. She left the situation alone for now, but in the back of her head, it wasn't over. She got ready for work without saying anything to Terrence and left. He sat right on the couch, turned the TV on and started watching the Channel 5 News.

Chapter 6

When Brooklyn got off work, she didn't go straight home. She went to The Red Moon Pub, a local bar to have a few drinks and try to clear her mind. She had a long day at work, and was still stressed overseeing Terrence coming out the bathroom with a stripper; the things she was imagining that was going on in that bathroom was driving her crazy. At work, the patients were giving her a hard time. She found out that the Nurse that comes in before her wasn't giving the patients their medication. So she was left with non-medicated psych patients and a big mess to clean up after the Charge Nurse was fired. She had a cup of coffee thrown at her by one patient that she was trying to give medication too. A drink for her was very overdue.

"Good evening, beautiful. How can I help you?" the bartender asked. She looked at him in a flirtatious way. He was fine. "You ok?" he asked her.

She shook her head. "I'm sorry. Yes, let me get an Adios, please."

"One Adios, coming up,"

"Thank you," she said, admiring his sexy, thinking, *"I need to come here and get drinks more often."*

"How's your day going so far?" the bartender asked as he placed her drink in front of her.

… "It's going cool," she hesitated and then she lied.

"That's good. Just getting off work?" he asked, looking at the coffee stain on her uniform shirt.

"Yeah had a long day,"

"I'll be with you in a second, sir," he told a guest at the bar. He looked at Brooklyn, "Well, I hope your day gets better, beautiful." he said and then walked off.

"Me too." she mumbled.

After sitting for a while and downing a few drinks, Brooklyn decided she would head back home…

***

As Brooklyn got in her car to head home, a text came through her phone from Terrence that read: **"Hey, where you at?"**

She sent a text back saying: **"Why, what's up?"**

She put her seatbelt on, started up her car, and drove off. As she maneuvered through traffic, an incoming text came through that read: **"Look, I'm sorry. What you say about us talking when you get here?"**

She texted back: **"Is that right, are you really? I guess. I'm on my way to the house, driving now, can't text."**

His incoming text read, **"Alright, I'll see you when you get here."**

"He bet not be up to any bullshit," she said to herself. After putting her phone down, she turned the volume up on her radio with Avant's *'Read Your Mind'* blowing through the speakers.

Was he going to give her the pity party? Would she forgive his disrespectfulness and abuse? As she drove listening to music and thinking, she thought back to when she and Terrence got into an altercation…

She did a lot of investigating and got his password to his Facebook account, logged into his account from her phone, and started going through his messages. The first message she clicked on was from,

Ms. Toobooty Tee, **"Wussup wit' cha'. If you are not doing anything later, slide through,"**

Terrence AllGas Carter: **"Alright, I'll see wut's up."**

Ms. Toobooty Tee: **"Ok, let me know."**

Terrence AllGas Carter: **"Fa' Sho',"**

"What?" Brooklyn thought heart in her stomach. *"This bastard!"*

She always accepted him back despite all the terrible things he'd done to her. He had her mind in the clouds, the sex was good like none other, and she would take him back *every single time.* It was hard for her to walk away, she felt some type of way about him. Growing up, she didn't have anyone to look up to in a positive way or that guidance that a female needed. At times, she would stop to think, *"What am I doing?"*

She exited out of his messages disgusted by what she was reading. Going through his Facebook menu, she scrolled down to, *'Groups'* he was in a sex group. She couldn't believe his *'Likes'* and *'Comments'*. Hurting, but eager to know more, she went back to his *'Inbox'*, going off the names in the *'Inbox'* the more interesting ones are the ones she would click on,

Hot Kitty Kree: **"Thanks for the gift. I got it today. Love you!"**

"What, a gift? Hell nah! Hot Kitty Kree." she said to herself screw faced.

Terrence AllGas Carter: **"U welcome, anything for my baby."**

"This nigga done lost his mind." When she looked at his profile it said, 'Complicated'. *"Complicated, really?"*

It seemed the more hurt he was doing to her, the more she loved him. *But why?* She could never figure it out. It was hard for her not to think of the wrong he did to her. *"One day, he will see my worth."*

Brooklyn didn't have a Facebook account. Well, she did have one; however, she deactivated it due to too much messiness and negativity that was on there. Facebook ruined a friend of her aunt's marriage, so she stayed away from it, only to log in to see his disrespectful, glad to know 'Complicated' relationship status, and his unfaithfulness. After doing some searching and investigating on, 'Hot Kitty Kree', she found out that, 'Hot Kitty Kree' was, Monica. For a couple of years, she and Terrence has been together, he and Monica had been having an on and off relationship with each other the whole time. Soon after, she found out about Monica's baby...

"Hello," Brooklyn spoke as she answered Terrence's phone. Somehow, she would always end up getting a hold of his phone. She was somewhat like an Investigator. She would find out anything. Where you work, your address, momma's address, whatever it was she would find out. Nothing was a secret with her.

"Is Terrence there?" the voice on the other end asked.

"Who's calling?"

"Is he there?"

"Really," Brooklyn thought. "Yeah, he here, but you're not speaking to him until you tell me who's calling,"

"Since you want to know so bad, this is, Monica."

"Monica? What you want with, Terrence? *What the hell.*" she asked and then thought.

"Since you insist, I want to tell him that I had our baby."

Silence… Brooklyn's mouth hung open. "His what?"

"Yeah, since you being all nosey all up in his shit, I just had his baby. So make sure you let him know, Hun."

Yes, Terrence got Monica pregnant and she refused to have an abortion, not that he stressed her about one, however, the question did come about. They had a little girl together, Aleena. Oh, how she was hurt, she wanted to have his first baby, his first girl. Still, after all, that, she took him back and accepted the fact that he had a baby on her. She felt so stupid. He would always win her back over by gifting her up. Jewelry, she loved her some gold. Top of the line clothes, money, or a new car. The material things kept her quiet many of the times. It was hard being with a person that cheated and lied all the time. *But what did she know? "Why keep it one hundred with a person if they not one hundred with you?"* she thought. Thoughts of cheating came to Brooklyn's head a few times, but every time she had the opportunity, she couldn't do it. Her guilty conscious would eat her up…

Shaking her thoughts, remembering she needed to get gas for in the morning, she pulled into the gas station to fill up, grabbed a Root Beer and a pack of Mambas, and continued home…

***

When Brooklyn walked in the door, all the lights were off, and Terrence was sitting in the dark on the couch, "Don't turn the light on, come here," he said patting the seat of the couch.

She took her shoes off at the door, sat her Grammercy Satchel bag on the living room table, and sat next to him. "What's up?" she said.

"Look, baby. I just want to say I'm sorry. I know my temper flare up pretty quick, but I'm working on it; I don't want to hurt you. Come here. Why you acting like that?" he said, grabbing her close.

She was acting a little standoffish. She was hurt and tired of him treating her the way he was. "You are putting me through too much, for no reason. How do I know you're not gone do the same thing?"

"Baby, I'm sorry. What else you want me to say. I can only show you. You know I love you, right?"

"I guess,"

He took her hands in his and gave her a kiss. She shied away. "Stop that," he told her.

"Stop what? You hurt me, Terrence."

"I know, baby, I know." He picked up a long, slim box off the table, opened it, took out an 18-karat Rose Gold Cuban Link bracelet, and placed it around her wrist where she had a tattoo that read, 'Terrence'.

"Oh my God," she thought. It was beautiful. Although she didn't want to show it, she loved it. She looked at him, then back down to the bracelet.

He then grabbed a second long box off the table. *"I can't stand him."* He opened the second box and placed an 18-karat Rose Gold matching link chain around her neck.

"You like it?"

She looked at him for a minute and then said, "It's cool." she responded with a smile on her face. She admired the bracelet and chain for a minute, his face, and then his chest. His body was amazing he stayed in the gym. His tone brought out his eyes, and he would always squint his eyes in a sexy way when he wanted his way. That worked many of the times too.

He brushed his tongue delicately against her neck. Her va-jay-jay throbbed, "Mm," she was weak for him. "I need to get in the shower first."

He didn't mind the wait. He was trying to win her back over. "Alright, go ahead. I'll be waiting."

She went into the bathroom and turned on the shower water, letting the bathroom steam for a minute while she gathered her belongings. Once in the shower, she felt relaxed as the hot water ran over her head, and down her body, and then leaned her head back with her hands over her face. *"Ah, this feels good."* she thought.

Terrence stood on the other side of the shower naked. He slid the shower curtain back and stepped in, grabbed her towel and squeezed her Pure Seduction body wash on it and began washing her up. He moved in close to her, reached around her, and began washing her back. He kissed her sensuously, soap dripping down her back to her ass. He caressed her gently as he washed her up. When he finished washing her up, she rinsed off. He stood back admiring her body, manhood at attention. She grabbed hold to the shower wall and braced herself as he lifted her leg to go down to lick her secret box. Her legs began to shake as he softly sucked on her pearl. He knew how to work his mouth good giving oral pleasure and just where to put his lips.

"Uh, huh, yeah, right there," she grabbed hold of his head. He would make her squirt her juices everywhere all the time. "You 'bout to make me cum," she said breathing sexy.

"Mm, mmm," he replied, mouth and lips occupied going in. One thing about, Terrence, he loved pleasing her orally. He knew she loved every bit of it.

After pleasing and taking in her sweetness, she washed and rinsed below and he carried her straight to the bathroom sink counter. He threw a towel on the floor to keep himself from slipping. To her, make up sex was the best and she just couldn't understand why. Once he was inside of her, she worked her hips fucking him back, pussy gripping his shiny long thick love muscle. They were fucking like 90 going west. After making her cum a few times, he picked her up, love muscle still inside and walked into the living room to the couch. They flipped positions with her now on top. She grabbed hold to his neck, arched her back, and rode him with him deep inside of her. The more he caressed, licked, and sucked on her 'C' cups the more her va-jay-jay throbbed.

"Who pussy is this?" he asked with a hard thrust.

"Ah, oh," she moaned.

"Who pussy is this?" he asked again.

"It's yours,"

"Well act like it then,"

"This dick feels good," she told him.

"Yeah, baby, I love it when you talk to me like that."

"Fuck me, oh, yes!"

"Baby, don't leave me," he said as they made love to each other. They were fucking and making love, it was something magical.

"I'm not." she responded softly.

"Uhh, uhh, ooh, you 'bout to make me cum again. Ah, shhh, shhh, mmm,"

"Take it, yeah. Oh, this pussy wet, oh, it feels good. Ah, ah, ah!"

Both their bodies shook as they came together. Breathing hard trying to catch their breath, they held each other tightly in each other's arms.

Chapter 7

Brooklyn was always being nosey. Well, to her it wasn't nosey, it was her intuition. She really loved Terrence and just couldn't put her finger on why he was doing her wrong. She was going to find out.

While chilling at the house with, Terrence, Brooklyn caught hold to his password to his voicemail. As he sat on the edge of the bed with his back turned to her getting ready to check his voicemail, she stood in the mirror doing her hair, not even trying to, but when she glanced back, she saw every number he typed in for his mailbox. That was all she needed and been waiting for.

"Did this fool just let me get a hold of his code?"

She used his code so that she could have access to his voicemail, and have every message that he receives sent to her phone. Even if he deletes his messages, she will still get them. Every time he gets a message notification, she would get one as well. The voicemails she was hearing, she couldn't believe it. Men will cheat, cheat, cheat, and never take the time to cover their tracks. Terrence was one of them, always getting caught slipping. Things had become a pattern with him. He became easy to read, he was like a book she wrote; she knew him from front to back. She knew all the games he played, she started playing the games right back along with him. She began to play right along at times just to see how far he would go with the lying and cheating.

After realizing their phones would go off together at times, Terrence said, "Why every time my phone goes off yours goes off?"

Brooklyn laid across the bed dumbfounded. "Huh? My phone doesn't go off every time yours go off."

"I must be tripping then,"

"Yeah, maybe so, it must be the weed. These phone companies and phones be tripping anyway, they always messing up," she said and then thought, *"Idiot."* She smiled in a mischievous way.

He never figured out that she was hearing and knew everything. Her heart was broken, how dare he.

***

While at home one day, Terrence phone went off constantly, ringing off the hook. Brooklyn knew it was something because he kept sending whoever it was to voice mail, and whoever it was left messages. In order for her to check the messages from her phone, she would block her number and call his phone. He never answered private calls, and at this time, he was probably thinking that it was just the person calling with a blocked number because he wasn't answering them.

Brooklyn grabbed her phone and went into the bathroom…

At the sound of his voicemail, she hit the star button. *"Please enter your passcode then press pound,"* Beep, Beep, Beep, Beep, she entered his four-digit code. *"You have three new messages."* She pressed one.

"Hey, baby, this Monica. Thanks for coming by yesterday. I'll be waiting for you tonight in my new white lace negligee."

She skipped the message; she would never delete them.

"Terrence, this Monica, you need to call me back. I need you to come keep Aleena; I have an appointment I need to go to."

"What, that's not even his damn baby," she thought, skipping to the next message.

"Aye, yo', T, hit Big Boy up."

She hung up the phone and was furious. *"So is it his baby or not?"* The things that he was doing to her were slowly pushing her away. When asked, Terrence would always deny that he was the father of Monica's daughter.

"Aye, Brooklyn, I'm about to hit a corner real quick," he yelled through the bathroom door. When he would 'Hit a corner' it will be hours before he came back home.

When she heard the door shut, she came out of the bathroom. Grabbed some weed off the dresser and rolled her up a blunt. She was a social weed smoker, and when she did smoke many of the times, it was by herself, to ease her mind.

After smoking, at least, half the blunt, Brooklyn got up out of nowhere and began rumbling through his things. She started feeling as if he was making her crazy. Maybe he was. She found a black leather wallet in the back of the drawer. Of course, she pulled it out. When she went through it, to her surprise, she stumbles over a picture of, Terrence, Monica, and her daughter. *"This bitch,"* she said aloud.

She went to work with a lot on her mind. Not able to focus, she left work a little early.

***

"Hey, girl, what you up to?" Brooklyn asked Brittney on the other end of the line. Kicked back with her feet up on her couch, Brooklyn sipped on a glass of wine.

"Nothing, in here cooking spaghetti… I thought you had to work. What's up?"

"Yeah, I did. I just left early, got a lot on my mind. So you cooked, good, I'm hungry anyway. I'm about to come by there."

"Girl, you are not about to come by here stop playing."

"Yes, I am, bye, see you in a minute." Brooklyn hung up the phone.

***

"You got it smelling good up in here," Brooklyn told Brittney, as she was welcomed in.

"You know I be doing my thing in the kitchen."

"You not better than me, though." they joked around.

"So what's up? You look like something is on your mind. What happened?" Brittney told her stirring up her ground turkey.

"Guess what?"

"What happened now?"

"Well, first, the good news is, I am about to start dating."

"Wait, what? Girl, shut up. You are not about to step out on Terrence."

"Just watch and see. I do have a little friend."

"So who is it?"

"His name is, Corey," she couldn't wait to say something.

"Corey, girl, who in the hell is, Corey?"

"He's a friend,"

"What about, Terrence?"

"What about him? Terrence is an asshole, and I'm getting tired of his ass."

"Mm, hmm, yeah right."

"I am, girl."

"So what's the deal with, Corey? You gave him the cookies?"

Brooklyn smiled. "No, he hasn't dipped in the goodies, yet."

"Well, okay," Brittney laughed. "Shit, I'll rather you be with anybody other than Terrence stankin' ass."

"Right, and hopefully it will push me all the way from his ass."

"Girl,"

"You better check those noodles,"

"Don't trip, I got this over here." She fanned her hand over the stove. "Have you talked to Aunt Bailey?"

"No, I haven't talked to her."

"Well, she talked to momma, and momma told her to see if we would want to meet with her."

"Meet with her? Meet with her for what?"

"She wants to apologize and see where it goes from there."

"I don't know. What did you say?"

"I said I have to think about it,"

After years passed, they still weren't sure if they were ready to forgive her.

"Yeah, let's think about it." they both agreed. "Anyway, girl, so, why in the hell I been doing some investigating, and, Monica's baby really is his."

"How you know?"

"Because it is and I saw her."

"You saw her, where? Don't tell me you went to that girl's house."

"No, I didn't. I heard messages and found a picture in his damn wallet that he had tucked deep away."

"What? So he has been lying this whole damn time?"

"Exactly,"

"What kind of man would deny his own child?"

"His ass be over her house and been taking care of the baby,"

"What! Wow, that's crazy. What you gone do?"

"I'ma leave his ass, I'm not about to keep taking his mess."

"That would be the best thing."

"Right," Brooklyn nodded up and down…

They both finished chatting and catching up. Brittney finished the spaghetti; they ate and said their byes.

Chapter 8

For years, Brooklyn stayed true to Terrence no matter what he did to her and how much he'd hurt her.

This one day, Brooklyn decided to take Corey up on his offer. She met him while with Terrence, they exchanged numbers, but never hung out. Brooklyn always came up with an excuse. Every once and a while, she would call him and he would call her. She told him she was in a relationship, however, wasn't happy. He wasn't in a relationship, but did admit to her that he was dating / seeing two different women. One thing that she liked about him was that he was up front from the start, something she could respect.

Corey was something nice. Smooth, shiny black goatee, thin almond eyes. He wasn't a male model, but he sure could have been. He was spontaneous with an adventurous personality. To Brooklyn, everything about him was right. She wondered why she didn't get with him earlier on. Oh, that's right; she was dedicated to Terrence, a man who continuously broke her heart. She met him at a gas station one day while pumping her gas.

"Excuse me, let me pump that for you," a male voice asked Brooklyn as she grabbed hold of the pump turning to stick the nozzle in her gas tank.

"Can you pump my gas?" she looked him up and down and laughed. "Are you kidding me?"

"What? I'm just being a gentleman, trying to help a sexy woman pump her gas. I don't see nothing wrong with that, I don't want no change, I just want your number," he said with a laugh.

She smiled flirtatiously. "Oh really, so you wanna pump my gas for my number?" they both joked around. "Well, here you go," she passed him the pump.

"So where yo' man at, sexy?"

"I don't know?"

"What you mean, you don't know?"

"He probably at home, who knows," she said fanning a hand.

"Oh, y'all must be on bad terms?"

"Something like that. Where is your girl at?"

"I don't have a girlfriend; I just have a couple friends."

"A couple friends, is that right?"

"Yeah, nothing serious, the single life," he finished pumping her gas replacing the pump. "So, you a nurse?" he asked, referring to her uniform.

"Yeah, I am."

"A sexy nurse in uniform… You can come help me when I get sick?" he said smiling.

"Really," The lame things men would say to a woman. "You are too much," she said with a giggle.

After small conversation and a few smiles, she gave in and they exchanged numbers.

***

After getting into an intense argument with Terrence over another one of his lies, Brooklyn left and went to her spot, The Red Moon Pub, once again to clear her mind.

"Hey, Brooklyn, how are you doing today?" Mike the bartender asked. As much as she stopped through there, all the workers knew her, and she knew all of them, including the owner.

"Hey, Mike. I'm cool. Let me get two shots of PATRÓN."

"Alright." he said, sitting two shot glasses in front of her.

After taking her two shots she phoned, Corey. "Hey, you," she said as he answered his phone.

"Hey, what's up with you, what happened?" he said and asked hearing her saddened voice.

"Oh, nothing, just got into it with this idiot again. What are you doing?"

"I'm just chilling at the pad. What's up?"

"I was calling you to take you up on your date offer," she told him straight out.

"My date offer, really? I see you made your mind up,"

"Yeah, I did,"

"I already told you, I'm available whenever you have time,"

"What are you doing later?"

"I don't have any plans; I'm free as a bird,"

"Alright, so how dinner and a movie sound, your treat?" she said with a smile.

"I can't believe you trying to come out and play,"

"Whatever, boy,"

"You gone come to me, I'ma come to you, what? How are we gone do this with your situation and all?"

"Okay, meet me on Slauson and Vermont in the Kmart parking lot, and I'll get in the car with you."

***

After meeting up, he took her to La Louisanne for some Creole food and drinks, and then to a movie. While at dinner, Brooklyn threw back a few shots. She was tipsy and feeling good, Corey, the same. The atmosphere was nice, dimly lit with Jazz music playing in the background while patrons ate and talked amongst each other. Corey and Brooklyn made small talk while waiting for a server to come to their table.

"I'll be back, I'ma go to the restroom," she told him getting up.

"You want me to order you something to drink?" he asked.

"Yeah, you can order me a shot of PATRÓN," She made that her drink for the day. As she walked to the restroom, she hoped she didn't run into someone she or Terrence knew. *"That will be my ass,"* she thought.

"Alright, mm," he said, watching her walk off.

Sexual thoughts went through her head. *"I want to take him down."* Before she even picked up the phone this day to call him, she had thoughts with intentions of giving him some of her cookies. She no longer gave a care about cheating; Terrence had pushed her to the limit of disrespect. She hoped that being with and hanging out with Corey on occasions would get her mind off Terrence, to one day leave him. She was drunk but knew exactly what she was doing. She was hot and wanted to give Corey what he been waiting for.

"There's your drink," he said, pointing when she came back from the restroom.

"Thanks,"

After ordering their food, Brooklyn filled him in on what she and Terrence had been going through. The only part she left out was, him physically abusing her. That was something he didn't need to know at the moment. It wasn't time for all of that.

"That's all bad. So why you still with him if he treating you bad?"

"At times, I ask myself the same thing,"

"I'm telling you, you need to come on this side of the fence and let me make you happy like you deserve,"

"Don't tempt me," she said jokingly, but was serious.

"I'ma leave that up to you,"

"What about your 'two friends'?"

"How about this, when you are serious, then I'll let them go,"

"Yeah, ok."

"I'm for real,"

"I bet you are."

"What you going to do after you leave here? You going back home?" he asked her.

"Nah, not in the mood to go there,"

"Well, want to come to my pad and kick it for a while, I promise you I won't bite,"

"Now that sounds like a good idea," she said without hesitation.

They both sat for a minute lusting over one another, imagining the sexual things they wanted to do with each other. The liquor had them thinking explicitly.

They enjoyed and finished their meals; he took care of the tab and took out a tip. "You ready to get out of here?" he asked her.

"Yeah, let's go."

They left and he took her to get her car. Once in her car, she hopped in her car and followed right behind him, in route to his house. While at a red light, she texts Corey, **"Make sure you tell your 'friends' that you will be occupied tonight."**

Her incoming text read, **"It's cool, sexy. It's just me and you with our phones off."**

She texted back, **"☺"**

***

"You have a nice house," she told him, admiring her surroundings. She stood in the middle of the living room floor. *"Nice couch,"* she said to herself.

"Get comfortable, don't be scared."

"Boy, ain't nobody scared. You decorated in here yourself?" she sat on the couch, took her shoes off, grabbed the TV remote off the couch, and turned the TV on.

"Yeah, I did. But the pictures were a gift."

The couch was in the shape of a 'U' with a rather low glass table in front. Above the fireplace was a huge Jackson Rustic Metal Mirror, with a Black Panther statue lying below.

"Where is your bathroom?"

"Right down here on the left."

When she came out the bathroom, she was being nosey. "So which room you sleep in?"

"The one right there where you standing at,"

"Want you show me around." She leaned against the doorway.

He walked up to her and pressed his lips against hers softly. It was right, how his lips connected with hers. "Oh, you got some soft lips," he told her.

"Thank you." speaking in between kisses.

He put his arm around her holding her close. Their soft, gentle kisses turned into more of a passionate one. He walked her over to his bed, laying her on her back, hands above her head. They wasted no time. He lifted her shirt over her head; spread her legs, now licking her lower abdomen near her panty line. He licked and played his tongue up to her soft plump lips. She gave it to him willingly. No one was there, but the two of them so who cared. He slipped his tongue between her lips, tongues intertwining. Driving his hand into her silk black hair, he grabbed it with his hand pressing her lips against his. Her body melted against his. Hunger emerged inside of him, eager to feel her warm insides. Brooklyn loved the feeling she was feeling, no stress, and no Terrence, finally. It felt good. She pressed herself against his chest, rubbing her hands up and down his smooth back. The touch of his hands and the feel of his body sent a burst of heat through her.

After so long, the material things didn't mean anything to Brooklyn coming from Terrence; that wasn't bringing her happiness anymore. She knew he was cheating, just didn't know for sure with whom and at times thinking it was multiple women.

Brooklyn was in the clouds for the moment; every sweet, soft kiss he placed on her while deep inside of her made her wetter and wetter until she came so hard; wetting his whole bed.

She chuckled. "I am so sorry; I wet your whole damn bed. She only came like that one time before, but this time, boy oh boy.

Corey laughed. "Don't worry about it, baby, I know he doesn't give it to you this good," he boasted.

The way she wet his bed, you would have thought water was poured on it. She got straight up and jumped in his shower. She didn't want any scent of Corey's on her. Leaving the door unlocked, Corey walked into the bathroom, grabbed a towel and soap to wash himself off, He wasn't worried about no shower right then.

"So, when I'ma see you again?" he asked her.

There was a pause... "Uh, I'm not sure; don't want to make any promises, but soon, though."

"Mm, hmm, don't let me come looking for you." They both laughed.

"Whatever, you will see me soon, trust me." She finished getting herself back together, and they said their goodbyes. He sent her out of there smiling from ear to ear, Terence was nowhere on her mind.

Chapter 9

"Um, we need to talk, sir," Brooklyn told Terrence.

He sat on the couch watching T.V as if he heard no one talking.

"So you're gonna sit there and act like you don't hear me?"

He looked around, "Did somebody say something?"

"Really, Terrence, you wanna play that game."

Terrence became a bastard, when he didn't want to hear it, he would try to ignore a person until they will give up. She hated that. *Where did his respect go?*

"Look, Brooklyn, don't nobody have time to be hearing your bullshit right now."

"My bullshit, no, you're with the bullshit! When you are gone man the fuck up and claim your shit?"

Blinded By Love

"Claim what shit, what the hell is your crazy ass talking about now?" What she was saying to him was irritating him so bad. "Look, now, gone with all that. You are driving yourself crazy." He shook his head and continued watching T.V.

She grabbed the remote control and turned the T.V off. "Do I have your attention now?"

"Brooklyn, turn the T.V back on and quit playing."

"You quit playing and explain this," She pulled out the picture of him, Monica, and their daughter and put it in his face.

He looked up, "Man where did you get that shit from?" As if it was a photo-shopped picture, she created.

She began to grow angry. "So you want her, is that it?"

She stood closer to him. "Step back some," he told her putting his hand out.

"No, I'm not moving anywhere. You need to explain this!"

"I don't need to explain shit. I'ma grown ass man," he tried to snatch the picture from her hand, but was unsuccessful because she snatched back quickly.

"You do have to explain if you with me! Why you can't be honest, be real, and man up. If she's your baby she's your baby, it ain't shit I can do about it. It will be my decision to leave or stay. Ugh! You a scandalous mother fucker,"

Terrence just sat there; what Brooklyn was saying, was once again, going out one ear and straight out the other.

"So you just going to ignore me like I'm invisible? You know what; fuck you and the pussy you came out of!"

"I'm outta' here, with your disrespectful ass!" He stood up, thought about it, and sat back down. It took all his might not to get up and knock her out. His mother was dead; however, she was hurting, how he expected her to feel. All the wrong,

65

disrespectful un-loyal things he did to her, her frustration was through the roof.

"Yeah, leave if you want to,"

"Man, gone. What's that supposed to mean?"

"It's sad you can't be a *Real Man* and tell the truth and take care of your responsibilities,"

"I do take care of my responsibilities. I take care of my daughter!"

"Oh, you admitting it now and claiming her?"

He laughed, "Oh, now it's a problem? Make your mind up, you either gone accept it or not?"

"Who the fuck you think you talking to? You are a real bitch who wasn't raised right!"

He jumped up so fast, went from zero to a hundred real quick, and punched the hell out of her. Brooklyn was stunned for a minute. "Speak on my momma again and call me another bitch, and you gonna be picking up yo' teeth from the floor.

"You have to go, you not about to keep putting your hands on me!" she said holding her face.

"Well stop always talking so much shit! Now, I said it's my baby, I take care of her, and that's that. It is what it is!

She cried, "Fuck you, Terrence! How could you do me like this? I gave you my all! You ain't right, you ain't right! I hate you!" She charged toward him swinging, punching and slapping him, and trying her best to dig in his face.

Terrence continuously tried to push her off him while blocking her hits. "Get your ass off me,"

"No, fuck y…" he slapped her to the ground before she could get her sentence out.

She got up to grab her phone, "If you don't leave, I'm calling the police."

"You not gone call shit, this my house too, I don't have to go nowhere." he stated, walking back and forth through the house while texting on his phone.

"Keep thinking I'm playing!" she picked up her phone and held it in her hand. She never called the police on him before, so why now. He didn't believe she would do it.

… Beep, beep, beep (911) she dialed on her phone. "911 operators this is operator thirty-five, what's the location of your emergency?"

Brooklyn started crying, "I need help, my boyfriend just beat me up and he won't leave."

"This bitch is really calling the police," Terrence thought.

"What's your address, mam?"

"One, 6…" as soon as she began to give the operator her address, Terrence, quickly started grabbing his shit so he can leave. He was not trying to be there when the police arrived. She continued giving her address. "Can you hurry, he is trying to leave now," she told the 911 dispatcher.

"Okay, mam, a squad car will be coming your way. I will stay on the phone with you until they arrive,"

Brooklyn held the phone to her ear in silence… Then she hung up in the operators face… Watching Terrence leave. He left; he left before the authorities could get there. She ran and locked the door behind him. Thought about it and then ran outside to see if she saw him anywhere around; he was nowhere in sight. By the time she got to the front gate, she saw a car driving off from the curve, but was unable to see the driver; it was the same car, a royal blue Acura, the one that had picked him up from his birthday party; the night he was caught in the bathroom with the stripper.

When the police arrived, she still gave them her statement word for word, telling everything about what had escalated. After they left, Brooklyn sat thinking, *"Who in the hell was in that car? I can't keep taking this. Will I be happier without him in my life? Do I really want to be here? Am I wrong, should I stay? Should I have called the police?"* A part of her felt somewhat bad for calling the police and another part of her said oh well fuck him. Thoughts, thoughts, and more thoughts went through her analyzing brain. She was stressed; she really wanted their relationship to work out and hopefully, get married and have kids, but the way, Terrence, was set up, that was impossible. But she had always kept her hope. Her heart would always tell her yes and her mind would tell her no. Her fault was she always listened to her heart thinking that was best. This time around, she chose to go with her mind. Her mind was made up, she decided to leave. The question was would she stick to it?

Chapter 10

When it came a time, Brooklyn backed out of testifying against, Terrence. She didn't want to take the stand, so the DA picked up the case.

After a few weeks went by, Brooklyn once again gave in; gave into Terrence's bullshit about how he'd been missing her, she is all that he wants, blah, blah, blah– The same song. She hadn't been calling him or returning his calls or text. One particular text she read from him was what got to her *Heart.*

No Good Bastard: **Baby, Brook, come on. I promise you I am sorry. I love you, want to marry you, and want you to have my baby. Please forgive me, I am sorry. I will even go to counseling. Just give me one more chance to prove myself.**

No Good Bastard was the name she had Terrence stored under. She let the message sit in her brain for some days. After talking to, Brittney, she still was thinking about taking him back. Her sister told her, to leave him, she could move in with her. She didn't need him, all he was doing was bringing her down. Brittney knew that her little sister could do better than him.

Brooklyn loved him and really didn't know why at this point. She also didn't want Monica to think she was winning. She felt she had put a lot in her relationship and didn't want all her hard work and dedication going to waste; all her invested time.

She went against her word and accepted him back, him, Monica, and the baby. *Was that something she really wanted to do?* Was she ready to take on that responsibility? Well, Brittney told her she was out of her damn mind, and to stop telling her what be going on with them if all she is going to do is take him back. She couldn't believe her sister. She just knew she was smarter than that. She could not understand why she kept taking him back. *His dick must be made of gold.* Brittney would think. Brittney couldn't make, control, or stop Brooklyn's final decisions; all she could do is give her advice and opinion, pray for her, and hope for the best.

Brooklyn had packed her some things. She had been staying with her sisters. Brittney knew something when she saw Brooklyn packing her bags. *"I know she's not,"* she thought, *"she better not go back to his ass."*

"I'm telling you, B, leave his scandalous ass alone. You don't need him; you can make it on your own."

"I know I can, but I love him. You don't understand he has been there for me when no one else has."

"So what, who fucking cares? Stop being so weak!" Brittney began to cry, "You not gone be satisfied until your ass is dead. Once an abuser always an abuser; I don't trust him and keep his ass away from me, and don't come crawling to me when he beats your ass or hurts you again." She went in on her, not caring how she felt about it.

"Really, Brittney, weak, how could you? He is going to get counseling and we are going to try to work things out. Nothing is going to happen to me."

"Yeah, that's what they all say."

They left the conversation at that. Brittney felt it wasn't any winning with Brooklyn at that moment, so she said no more. *It was her life.* She stayed the rest of the day at Brittney's and later left to go back home.

***

Before Brooklyn went home, she told Terrence, the only way she would come home and be with him was if he would marry her. *Was she serious? What was going through her mind?* She was taking a big chance.

When Brooklyn made it home, Terrence wasn't there. She scanned the house for any signs to see if a woman had been there. She searched his things just to make sure he wasn't hiding anything or if anything suspicious would be laying around. Usually, when she searches, she finds something, but this time around, she didn't find anything. If it was anything, he cleaned up very well. She proceeded to unpack her bags to put her things back up. She got in the shower thinking to herself, was Terrence, ready to stop playing childish games, and get his mind right. After showering and getting fresh, she slipped on something comfortable; she had on her turquoise, black, and gray Joe Boxer pajama set, smelling fresh of the scent of pure paradise. She slipped on her slippers and headed into the kitchen to cook up a meal. She made baked chicken breast with garlic, bell peppers, sweet onions, homemade gravy, white rice, broccoli, and sweet garlic rolls.

"Damn, it smells good in here. I sho' been missing that." Terrence said as he walked in the door.

"Hey, yeah, I bet you have. You not gone ever find someone who can make it taste good and smell this good like me," she told him, smiling.

He walked in the kitchen, "Can I have a hug?" he asked her as she turned from putting the butter back in the refrigerator.

She turned and looked at him with a smirk, "I guess,"

"Why you have to guess?" he stood admiring how her curves stood out in her fitted pajama pants.

She looked at him up and down and couldn't believe how much she had been missing him. She finally reached in and gave him a hug; they held each other tightly.

"Baby, I'm sorry," he whispered in her ear.

"Is that so?"

"Yes, I *promise* I will not hurt you again."

"Don't break any *promises* this go round because I will not be taking it *lightly*," she told him. *"Damn, he smells good."* She thought to herself while he held her in his arms.

"I'm serious, it's me and you."

"I'ma hold you to that." She said, loosening up her grip releasing their hug. "Well, the food is ready if you are hungry."

"Alright, let me take my shower real quick."

"Ok."

While Terrence was in the shower, Brooklyn warmed up the food and grabbed a bottle of peach CÎROC out the cabinet. The whole time she was thinking— she had felt a little uneasy for a moment, something just didn't feel right. *Or was she just tripping?*

Terrence walked out the bathroom looking sexy as always, wearing a pair of gray and red polo pajama pants with no shirt, smelling like YVES SAINT LAURENT La Nuit De L'Homme from head to toe. Brooklyn looked up and couldn't do anything but picture herself licking and slurping him down on top of the dinner table.

Terrence cleared his throat, bringing her out of her daze. "Looks like you hungry for something," he told her.

"Yeah, I am, hungry for this good food I made."

"Mm, hmm, if you say so,"

She jumped up, grabbed the two plates she had sitting on the counter, prepared them, and sat them on the table. They both sat at the table to eat and began to have small conversations. While in the middle of them eating, Terrence got up, went to the room, came right back out and sat back down at the table. Before she knew it, Terrence was in front of her on bended knee, with a sparkling diamond engagement ring in his hand.

Her eyes got watery; she couldn't believe that he was down on one knee. *"Is he serious?"* she thought.

"Baby, please give me one more chance to make this here right. Please don't say no, I am so sorry," he told her apologetically. He sounded very sincere he was sorry, regretful. *Was it enough to win her over?*

"Oh my God, Terrence, is this really real? Don't play with me. You know I have been waiting for this for a long time now."

"Yes, baby, I'm very serious; so, are you gone say yeah, or what?" he said with a smile.

"Yes, yes!" she reached in hugging him. A tear fell from her eye. He picked her up and carried her to their room. They forgot all about the rest of their food. They were just hungry for each other.

After undressing, he wasted no time. As he was standing, he picked her up pushing his stern pipe in her sweet wetness. She inhaled and exhaled, "Ah, hhh!" She tightened her grip around his neck. He held her by her ass, bouncing her up and down, as her juices splashed out on him. She was loving the 'D'. He gave it to her good; had her legs shaking the whole time. He knew just what she liked, and he was giving it to her just the way she liked it.

Make up sex, are you kidding me, that shit was explosive. She loved how he would take control when it went down in the bedroom.

Chapter 11

A month later, Terrence and Brooklyn tied the knot. Brittney was pissed. To her, her sister signed her life over to the Devil. They didn't have a big wedding, they headed down to the Registrar's Recorder/County Clerk's building. Although Brittney was invited, she did not attempt to go. She lied, telling Brooklyn, she was not able to take off work.

Terrence sat in the living room, feet propped up, and texting on his phone when Brooklyn walked in with a gift box in her hand.

"Here you go," she said, extending the gift.

He looked up, "What's this for, it ain't my birthday, we just got married, so it's not our anniversary." he told her.

"I know it's not, here just take it, before I take it back."

He took the gift and opened it, and to his surprise, it was a positive pregnancy test. He took it out the box and stared at it.

"Congratulations!" she told him smiling.

"I know this is not what I think it is?"

"What, you not happy? I thought you wanted a baby," she said, smile turning into a frown.

"Oh, no, I am happy. I'm just surprised, that's all. Come here," he told her, grabbing her close hugging her.

She sat next to him on the couch. "How far along are you?" he asked her.

"Well, I'm not sure yet. I just bought a pregnancy test and took it, because I missed my period. I have to make a doctor's appointment and then I will know for sure." Her phone went off, she looked at it and placed it face down. It was, Corey. It went off again and she turned it off.

"Who is that blowing you up?" he asked.

"That's Brittney, she wants me to ride with her somewhere," she told him, lying.

"So you ready for a baby?" he asked her.

"Yeah, I am. I'm excited. You don't seem too happy." she said, looking over at him.

"I am, so don't keep saying it." Terrence got up, "I'll be right back. I have to make a quick run real quick. Got a shipment coming through the Laundromat, and I don't fully trust this new worker, I have just yet."

She turned her lip up. "Okay, I guess we'll talk more about it when you get back, then."

"Alright," He kissed her on the forehead and left.

***

Once Terrence was long gone, Brooklyn returned Corey's call. "Hey, what's going on?" she asked when he answered.

"Oh, now you wanna call. You were forwarding me to voicemail a while ago."

"I was talking to, Terrence about something."

"About what?" he asked.

"Well,"

"Well, what? What is it? I thought we were keeping it real with each other?"

"We are,"

"Well, why it's taking you so damn long to say something?"

"If you give me a chance and stop jumping down my throat, I might be able to tell you."

"Alright, well tell me when you ready." he said with a little attitude.

"I told him I am pregnant,"

"You what, pregnant, so what did he say?"

"He didn't really say too much, I guess we will talk about it when he comes back. He didn't seem too happy, though."

"How you know it ain't mine?" he asked concerned.

"What do you mean?"

"You know what I mean; it could be a chance that it could be mine."

"Nah, it can't be."

"Well, what if I wanted to know for sure for myself?"

"Really?" she thought. "You will just have to take my word for it."

"And what if I don't want to take your word for it?"

"Then you will just have to wait until I have it and have a blood test done. But I'm telling you now that I know for sure that it's Terrence's baby."

"Yeah, okay, we will just have to wait and see. When you coming through, or do the police have you in handcuffs and you can't get free?"

She chuckled a bit, "Shut up, ain't anybody got any handcuffs on me. Give me a minute; I'll call you when I'm pulling up. Let's go out somewhere, I feel like getting away."

"Alright, see you in a while." he told her, and then hung up.

Although she knew for sure that Terrence was the daddy, she still pulled up her calendar on her phone to add up her days just to double check. She didn't know why she let Corey get in her head with the bull. *But what if it was Corey's baby, what would she do?*

Throughout her pregnancy, she went back and forth between, Terrence and Corey, with Terrence full time and keeping Corey on the side. Corey didn't mind, he knew what was up from the jump. After accepting Terrence back, she never dedicated her all to him. She had already grown feelings for Corey. She wanted to have her cake and eat it too. From being treated how she was treated, she didn't think what she was doing was wrong. That other uncaring side of her said, *do you, he had a baby on you, don't worry about him.* She hated at times when that side would come out, but at the same time loved it, because she was able to do things that the nice side of her wouldn't do; giving her a sense of relief. The uncaring not so nice side would say, she wouldn't mind her baby being Corey's, so she could get rid of Terrence's no good ass.

Brooklyn didn't have any intentions of getting her feelings involved with, Corey. She wanted to remain, friends, friends with benefits. However, throughout them seeing each other, they did grow closer.

This night, Terrence stayed the night out once again. When the clock struck 12 a.m., she knew he wasn't coming home. She called his phone, no answer. *"Fuck him,"* While Terrence was out doing him and whatever else− Brooklyn, would do the same behind his back. Two wrongs don't make it right, but hey, she was only human. She decided to no longer sit around and play the victim. By spending time with Corey, it was making a part of her happy. They would go out and do different things, dinner, working out, movies, cruises, clubs, etc. Whatever made her happy they did it; he brought out a side in her that she didn't even know she had. He brought out her spontaneous side. She felt free around him, he paid her attention, attention that, Terrence was lacking.

Chapter 12

"Hey, Brittney, what you doing?"

"Hey, sis, nothing, just got finished playing cards with, Paul. What's up?"

"I know you are going to feel some type of way,"

"Some type of way about what?"

"I'm pregnant,"

"Brook, really! Now you know…"

Brooklyn cuts her off, "I know, I know. But I want to keep it, and I am going to keep it."

"So who's the daddy?"

"Really, Britt?"

Brittney laughed, "I'm just saying, you *are* fucking two different men."

"Whatever, shut up. I called to talk to you, not for you to talk down to me."

"I'm just messing with you, girl, stop being all up in your feelings. I'm going to be here regardless."

"Thanks,"

"Anyway, I was going to tell you that, I set a date, time, and place for us to meet up with, Bridgette." They didn't even call her momma anymore, she had to earn that back.

"Why, for what? That lady doesn't give a damn about us, Brittney."

"I just feel everybody deserves a chance. You are about to have a baby, now, you should want her to be a part of that and want your baby to get to know her. Maybe the baby will bring us closer."

"Yeah, I understand, but."

"Okay, look, let's just try this one time. You will be able to tell if she is real or not. If she is really sorry, you know."

"Let me sleep on it,"

"Yeah, don't be sleeping too long."

"You get on my nerves,"

"That's what I'm here for, bye."

***

Bridgette invited Brooklyn and Brittney out to lunch. Brittney was all for it. She figured, hell that was a long time ago, wounds heal, and furthermore, it is her momma. She wouldn't be here if it wasn't for her. *You live and you learn, you forgive and move on.* It took Brooklyn some time to accept, a part of her really didn't want to, but that damn nice side of her wanted to. It was just hard for her to understand.

They talked over lunch. In the beginning, Brooklyn's shield was all the way up, she couldn't believe that she was sitting across from her mother, the lady that let her get abused. The day before she met with her, she read some scriptures from her bible…

Matthew 6:14-15
[14]For if you forgive men when they sin against you, your heavenly Father will also forgive you.
[15] But if you do not forgive men their sins, your Father will not forgive your sins.

Ephesians 4:31–32
[31]Let all bitterness and wrath and anger and clamor and slander be put away from you, along with all malice. [32]Be kind to one another, tenderhearted, forgiving one another, as God in Christ forgave you.

She asked God for guidance and strength throughout their meeting. "All I want to know is why?" Brooklyn asked.

Bridgette started off by saying, "I'm not going to just come out and apologize because I have already done that and people need to show and prove. So I just want to explain myself. I know I wasn't there for you guys like I should have been, but I was stupid and let a man overpower me and get in my brain. No one ever told me to watch out for this man and that man. I didn't have guidance when growing up, no one even taught me about my period; how long to keep on my pad, when to change my pad– I learned it all on my own, I'm not making any excuses, I'm just saying I lacked knowledge of certain things. And I have learned from that, I have been saved and I'm always in church. If I could do it over, I would do it over in a much better way, I would not make the bad choices that I made." She went on asking and begging for their forgiveness. She asked for a fresh start a do over, she wanted to show them that she had really changed for the better.

They sat there and heard her out, giving her the floor to pour her heart out; they both felt that she was very sincere and apologetic; they just knew it would take some time to rebuild from the ground up... They all reminisced and cracked a few smiles, for the first time in their lives, they actually missed her, but they didn't tell her that. They told her that they are open to working things through with the help of a counselor.

Brooklyn told her the news that she was pregnant, but didn't fill her in on any detail, she wasn't comfortable with her just yet to tell her anything, really.

"So am I getting a baby shower invite?" she asked.

"You should, but it's too early for invites right now."

Brittney looked over at Brooklyn and shook her head. They finished their lunch and promised to keep in touch.

Chapter 13

Seven months into Brooklyn pregnancy, Terrence took her by the neck and slammed her to the floor, "Fuck you, you fat bitch! Nobody gonna want your fat outta shaped ass!"

Sharp pains shot through her stomach; she couldn't think of nothing but her daughter that she was carrying. Her stomach was huge and it was no way she could really protect herself. Brooklyn held onto her stomach and tried to get up, "Fat... nigga, you sound stupid...," she yelled out in pain.

Brooklyn began to lift herself off the floor before she could get all the way up, *"BOOM..."* Terrence kicked her dead in her side, knocking her back down to the floor. He put his size nine feet on her stomach with pressure, holding her down.

"Get your fucking foot off my stomach, you're hurting my baby!" she cried, squirming trying to push his foot off her. She was in so much pain; at that moment, it felt as if she were going to lose her baby.

"This nigga is really trying to hurt me," she thought.

"Fuck you and that mutha' fucking baby; I know it ain't mine anyway!" Terrence yelled out.

Grabbing her by her hair, he pulled her off the floor, threw her on the bed, and straddled himself atop of her. Before he could get her hands held down good, she hit him twice, once in the nose and once to his jaw. "Bitch…" he bellowed and then socked her in her eye. Her eye began to close up, and soon after started to swell.

"Ah, get off me; get your punk ass off me!" She was trying her best to get him off her. She took all the strength that she had left in her, and kicked his ass so hard, sending him off the bed and into the wall.

"Oh shit!" she said to herself.

She didn't know what was to come, so, she hurried and jumped off the bed, and ran into the bathroom. Before Brooklyn could get the door closed shut, Terrence had stuck his hand in the doorway to keep the door from closing shut.

"Move your hands out the way!" she yelled panicking.

Terrence was trying to push his way into the bathroom, and she was trying her best to keep him from coming in; she knew if he got in it was over for her. He was pissed about how hard his head hit the wall from that good kick she gave him. He wouldn't move his hands out the way of the door, so she bit the shit out of his fingers…

"Fuck! Ah!" he yelled so loud. I know for sure that the neighbors heard it.

The adrenaline in Brooklyn felt so good from hearing him in such pain. *"Bitch ass nigga."* she thought devilishly.

He couldn't do anything but move his hands. She slammed the door and locked it. *"Fuck, I can't keep going through this shit."* She looked in the mirror at her swollen busted eye.

"Bitch, open this mutha' fuckin' door! Yo' ass can't stay in there all night!"

When Brooklyn looked in the mirror, all she saw was a weak person with low self-esteem who didn't know what to do with herself. She knew if she stayed in there long enough eventually he would leave. Brooklyn was just a battered woman with a good heart, *'Blinded by Love'.*

"Now look what you made me do, all I wanted was some pussy, that's all!" Terrence had a long hard day at work after he found out one of his runners came up short from the batch he was supposed to get off while also finding out that one of his side pieces was pregnant. After trying to bribe her and talk her into getting an abortion, and her final answer was, No! Yep, he just couldn't do right, he was still dipping into things he had no business. The rest of his day didn't go so well. After work, he stopped off and got him a fifth of Hennessey, no chaser; and took it down. "I know you fucking somebody else," he told her beating on the door. Terrence was drunk as hell and out of his mind; he was tripping.

"Terrence, I told you over and over again that I am not fucking with anybody. You are fucking crazy. I'm seven months pregnant, what the hell I look like? My body be tired at times!" she cried out. "You told me you were going to change, this doesn't look like a change!"

"I have changed. Baby, just come out and we can talk about it. I'm sorry," Terrence, pleaded as if he was bipolar. He was just in a rage and now cool, wanting to talk it out. "I'm sorry, baby."

Terrence would sing the same old song all the time. In Brooklyn's heart, she knew what she was going through was not right. However, in her mind, she could not leave that man. He had her mind gone and her nose wide open. When they weren't fighting, he would show her nothing but love and cater to her. All her life that's what she wanted, someone to just love her and show her that they cared. He knew that about her and knew she really didn't have anyone else. She had her sister, but after so long she stopped getting involved in their relationship, because all Brooklyn would do is go crawling right back to him. Plus, after he went off on Brittney and told her to get out of their house, she stopped coming around as much. She too was having her own relationship issues; however, they weren't as bad as Brooklyn's.

Brooklyn started feeling hard, sharp pains in her stomach from the beating she received. After hearing a door slam, what sounded like the front door and silence for about fifteen minutes, she crept out the bathroom. "Ahh," she moaned in pain, holding her stomach, looking around making sure he was gone; there was no sign of him. She went and sat on the couch hoping that the pain will go away, but it didn't it got worse. She felt something warm and slippery between her legs, so she put a hand down there, when she looked at her hand, it was blood on it; she panicked. She then began to cry harder. She got up slowly grabbed her keys and headed to the hospital. While on her way to the hospital, the pains in her stomach were coming harder, feeling like contractions. *"Oh my God, please help me!"* she cried. *"It's gone be ok, baby, just hold on."*

Chapter 14

Brooklyn was finally at a zero tolerance with, Terrence. He disgusted her already. After losing her baby, that was it. She packed up her things and beyond any doubt, she was ready to leave until she found bank statements and important papers that belonged to him in a manila envelope sticking out from behind his dresser. She rambled through the papers and stumbled over a marriage certificate with Monica and his name on it. When she saw the marriage certificate, her heart stopped, dropping to her stomach. She couldn't believe what she was seeing. *"How I miss all this?"* she questioned herself. *"This sneaky bitch!"* she said out as she looked through the papers. Terrence always had money, and she would always say, "Why won't you get a bank account instead of having all this drug money on you."

However, in return his response would be, "Nah, I'm good. I don't trust banks." While all the time he already had an open account. She was thinking she was the only one with a secret account. The marriage wasn't sitting to cool with her. But she wasn't going to say anything about it to him. The more she looked through the papers, the more pissed she became. He and Monica was planning to skip town together!

She made him an online account with his bank so that she could keep up with every deposit and withdrawal he makes. When she checked his account, he had four hundred thousand dollars in his checking account. After setting up the account and being nosey, she placed the papers back in the envelope and put it back, behind the dresser as if it was never touched. She unpacked all her stuff she had packed up and ready to go, putting everything back where it belonged before Terrence made it back.

With him knowing how nosey she was, he would always keep his personal things in different places. When he found out she was quick to pack his belongings or destroy his property, he stopped hiding things in the closet and in his shoeboxes. One day, Brooklyn burnt and cut up his clothes, burning up two thousand dollars he had in his clothes stashed away.

After inheriting two hundred thousand dollars from his mother's insurance policy, Terrence thought, *"Damn, two hundred thousand dollars, shit!"* He didn't know what he was going to do with that much money. Of course, he was thinking of opening up a bank account. He wouldn't dare keep that amount of money in his possession. He headed over to Bank of America to open up and deposit his check. He deposited all of it, every penny, also depositing money that he was making on the side. No one even knew he had it, and that's how he wanted it to stay.

Terrence let his money sit untouched in the bank for a good six to eight months before he touched it. After withdrawing one hundred and fifty thousand dollars, he connected with a distributor that had pure Black Tar in Sinaloa, Mexico, purchased two kilos out of it, and splurged off the rest. His product was so pure, the people on the streets were loving it, they called it, 'Black China' After tripling his money, that's when he invested some of his money in owning his own Coin Laundry; using it to launder money and drugs.

Brooklyn couldn't get her mind off that marriage certificate, as bad as she wanted to say something about it, she kept it to herself not telling anyone. *Now, what was she going to do?*

***

First, she began to send out a text, and then she erased it and dialed the number instead. "Hey, Monica, this is, Brooklyn," she spoke when she answered.

Brooklyn contacted Monica to invite her out to lunch so they could talk and try to work things out between them; thinking that would keep a lot of the drama down between the two. Monica would at times throw her daughter, Aleena in Brooklyn's face and would at times use her against Terrence.

"Uh, huh," Monica responded.

"I know this might sound crazy, but, I was wondering if you wanted to go out for lunch so that we can squash this nonsense at least for, Aleena," she said in a convincing way.

"Um, I don't know about all that."

"Look, I'm not trying to be Aleena's mother, if that's what you're thinking. I'm just tired of going through this bullshit. I don't need all this back and forth unnecessary drama in my life."

Monica didn't know what to think about the situation, especially with having trust issues with women. She definitely wasn't trying to make Brooklyn a friend. She sat for a minute thinking about Aleena being around her. *Did she really want that?*

"Let me think about it for a minute and I'll let you know later on today."

"Okay, that's fine."

Will Monica take the bait or not? She did, the offer was extended and she took it. *"Why not? If this bitch is going to be around my daughter, what the hell."* she thought.

Chapter 15

Monica laid in her bed all day in pain. She was feeling fatigue; she had a headache, was dizzy, vomiting, was having back pain, and was having bad abdominal pain. She didn't know what was wrong. She was hoping that she wasn't pregnant because another baby by Terrence was something she just didn't want. She told herself that if she is feeling the same tomorrow after taking some over the counter MEDs, she would try to make her way to her doctor or emergency room, whichever will take her first.

"Hey, Terrence, what's up?" Monica spoke into the phone.

"Nothing, just got in the house. What's up?"

"I haven't been feeling too good, and I wanted to know if you could come pick Aleena up so I can get some rest," she told him in an exhausted tone.

"Um…" he responded not really in the mood. "I don't know how Brooklyn would feel about that." As if, he really cared. Terrence didn't care about nobody but himself, needs, and wants.

The crazy part was, these women would still have sex with him and do anything for him no matter how he treated them. Being so 'Blinded' they looked past the bad things, continuing to love him.

"Really, Terrence, she is your daughter too. I didn't lie up and make her by my damn self. I'm fucking sick and weak, please. Fuck how Brooklyn feels, if she can't accept that you have a child, you don't need to be with her. I talked to her already anyway and we supposedly had worked it out."

"Oh, so you talked to Brooklyn?" he asked not believing her. As much as they hated each other, it was hard for him to believe.

"Yeah, I talked to her. We went out to lunch and talked things through like grown women. So man up, act like a man, and come get your daughter!"

"I am a fucking man, don't sit up and act like I don't take care of my daughter. How you think she got all that shit over there," he stated, referring to all of her clothes, shoes, and toys.

"That's material shit, fucked that. What about spending quality time with her? That's what she needs." Terrence was doing the same thing to Aleena that he was doing with Monica, Brooklyn, and whomever else he was messing around with, not spending time and being there for her physically. He would just throw materialistic things at her to keep her happy.

"I'll be there in a minute just have her stuff ready when I get there."

"Okay, thanks, Terrence."

Terrence didn't respond, he just hung up the phone.

***

"Aye, what's up? Why you didn't tell me you and Monica went out to lunch to work some shit out?" Terrence asked.

"Oh, and hello to you too; I was gone tell you, I guess it slipped my mind. Why, what's up? I see she told you. What did she say? And why you so worried about it and mad, what you think she gone tell me something that I don't need to know?"

"I ain't worried about that shit. I ain't got shit to hide," he said, lying as if he always tells the truth.

"Mm, okay. So what's up?"

"I'm about to go pick up my daughter and bring her to the house,"

"Oh, really, what happened? I guess our little talk worked."

"She said she sick and need me to keep her until she gets better."

"Keep her until she gets better? What you know about taking care of a child? You can't even sit in one place for too long."

"That's what I got you for,"

"Mm, is that so? I guess." Brooklyn responded, and then thought, *"He must think everything is just peaches… Mm-hmm,"*

"What you mean, I guess? I thought y'all were cool?"

"We are. But at the same time, she is no friend of mine, and shit we ain't that damn cool that fast. And you need to understand that this is going to take me some time to get used to. It's not that easy you know. You just threw this shit in my face, give me a fucking break. And why she sick anyway, you got her pregnant *again?*"

"Whatever man, hell no, she ain't pregnant. I'm about to go over there real quick and pick her up."

"Yeah, ok." she stated and hung up the phone.

***

Monica walked into the Emergency Room and sat at the first empty window, she saw a receptionist sitting and looking as if she needed to be working.

"Yes, how can I help you?" the receptionist asked.

"I have been throwing up and I can't keep anything down. My stomach is cramping and I am having bad migraines."

"Are you pregnant?"

"No, no I'm not."

"How long have you been having these symptoms?" she asked passing her a clipboard with a few forms attached. "Here, fill this out for me, please."

"I've been feeling like this for like a day or so."

"Okay, I will need your I.D and insurance card,"

Monica pulled her information from her purse and slid it through the window with the forms she had filled out.

"Ok, thank you, mam. Have a seat over in the waiting area and wait to hear your name."

"Thanks. Is it going to take a long time?" Monica asked. A hospital was not the place she wanted to be sitting. She was tired; feeling drained, and just wanted to lay in her bed.

"I'm not sure, but it shouldn't be that long. I don't want to give you a definite time, and don't call, and then you come up here mad at me," the receptionist explained, nicely.

"Right, I understand." Monica told her, and then said to herself, *"Yeah, because you will get cursed the hell out!"* She stood up, "Okay, thanks," she looked around; she was hearing coughing, a few people didn't even have the decency to cover their mouths or even cough into their elbow. People were sneezing, and kids were crying. *"Ugh!"* she said to herself, having to settle for an empty seat that was next to a pregnant girl with a black eye and a baby on her lap. She sat down and put her head down in her hands.

***

About two hours later,

"Monica Burris!" a Triage Nurse called from the intake room door.

Monica got up. *"Finally, shit."*

"Have a seat here," She pointed to a chair sitting next to a blood pressure machine.

After her intake, she was taken to the back and from there she was admitted into her own room. What was going on?

Monica laid in a hospital bed watching the Channel 7 News with an I.V in one hand and a blood pressure cuff attached to her other arm. Confused as to what was going on with her, she had no idea what could have been going on with her body. All they had told her was that she was very dehydrated and had a virus. The sickness just came out of nowhere…

"Hi, Monica, how are you? I'm Doctor Pullen," he said as he walked in her room.

She looked at him and nodded her head. "It feels like I am getting worse,"

"We are going to keep you overnight. We are running some labs and they are taking a little while to come back. So we want to keep you here under observation."

"Overnight, what you mean? My baby, I have to get home to my daughter," she cried to him.

"We can't just let you leave under your conditions. Moreover, you will turn around and be right back in here. Let us find out what is causing you to have these symptoms. Mam, you are in good hands, we are going to do our best to take care of you."

Monica looked up and rolled her eyes. "Alright, I guess."

"I'll be in here as soon as the results come in."

"Ok. Thank you, Doctor."

Monica picked up the phone and called, Terrence. "Hey, T, I am still at the hospital and they are keeping me overnight."

"What? What did they say?"

"They not sure yet, but they do know I am dehydrated and have a virus."

"A virus, what kind of virus?"

"Shit, Terrence, I don't fucking know!" she answered irritated. "I hope it ain't no damn cancer or no fucking AIDS," she said scared and worried.

"AIDS! Cancer! Man, shut that shit up. You just got the flu or something, ain't nothing no MEDs can't cure."

"Well, it's scary not knowing what's wrong with you."

"You're gonna be alright,"

"You have to keep Aleena, please."

"Yeah, yeah, I got you. I'll be up there tomorrow afternoon, I'll bring Aleena too."

"Ok. Thanks, I really appreciate this."

"Alright, take care." he told her and then hung up.

"Shit." Monica laid back, lifted the foot of her bed thinking and eventually dozed off."

Chapter 16

Terrence had to explain to Brooklyn, why Aleena had to stay the night. She didn't get upset and had welcomed her with open arms. *"We were going to have to get to know one another one day, so why not start with this day."* Brooklyn thought. Terrence couldn't believe how Brooklyn was so accepting.

"I'ma take Aleena to the hospital so she can see her momma," Terrence told Brooklyn.

"Mm hmm," she responded as she sat in her bed Indian style reading *Hood Girlz 2. Her* eyes glued to the pages of the book; she could care less what he was talking about, she was trying to find out what was about to happen to Slim; if he was going to jail or not.

He looked at her, "Man that book can't be that damn good." He wasn't much of a reader.

She looked up, "If you say so. Read it and see for yourself. It might help your ass sit still," she told him.

"You got jokes, huh?"

"Nah, I'm serious." she said and then continued reading.

"Alright, I'll be back," He and Aleena headed off to the hospital.

Brooklyn shook her head and kept reading.

***

Monica got worse overnight. *"It doesn't take this damn long for results to come back."* She was having difficulties with her breathing, feeling dizzy, having diarrhea; she was feeling weaker and having blurry vision.

Terrence walked into her room carrying, Aleena. "Damn, you look bad."

"Hi, to you too, give me my baby," she told him, holding out her arms. He passed her Aleena and she hugged her as tight as she could. "Mommy loves you," she told her as a tear fell from her eye. She hurried and wiped her face, "How was she?" she asked Terrence.

He pulled a chair close to her bed and sat down. "She was cool. You just got her spoiled."

Monica smiled. "Um, it seems like I am getting worse. Do you think you will be able to help me out with her until I get better or is it going to be a problem?"

"It should be cool," he said, looking at Aleena. "I can get used to her being around."

"Is that so?" Monica cracked a smile.

Chyna S.

Dr. Pullen walked in, "Hey, Ms. Burris, how are you feeling?" he asked.

"Not good. Have my results come in yet?" she sat up in her bed.

"As a matter of fact, they have, I have them right here." He looked over at Terrence.

"It's ok, Doctor, he is my husband and my child's father."

"Okay, mam, if you insist," he told her, and then proceeded, "according to my exam and the test results, you are suffering from respiratory failure."

Monica's mouth hung low, she couldn't believe that this doctor was standing in front of her telling her, her system was failing. "I... I what? What in the hell does that mean?" she questioned. She had no idea what respiratory failure was, she just knew it didn't sound good. All her life she had been healthy, no diseases; nothing.

Terrence was just sitting there quietly. He didn't even know what the doctor was talking about. But just from the look on the doctors face, he knew whatever it was it wasn't good. He didn't want to say the wrong thing, so he just listened.

"Monica," the doctor said, "you might not be able to breathe on your own, and will eventually need to be put on a respirator."

She put her head back; tears began to fall down her sad looking face. *"What the fuck is this crazy ass man standing here saying to me? He can't be serious, this has to be a dream and I will be waking up soon."* She blanked out and went into a deep thought, seeing nothing but black.

"Monica," a deep voice called. *"Don't worry, let me handle this. Give it to me and I will take very good care of you!"* Chills went through her body.

"Ms. Burris are you ok?" the doctor asked. "Ms. Burris!" he called. She sat up slowly. "How are you feeling?" he asked.

She shook her head, "Not good. I'm scared, doctor, I am really scared, respiratory failure? How, like, I mean, where did it come from? I was fine, I was feeling just fine," she cried.

"Your AST and ALT blood levels are out of range; they are high, your liver is damaged." Her heart dropped quickly. "The good thing is, it is not too late to treat you. However, you will have to be put in a medically induced coma. We need to find the root to this. Pretty soon your lungs and heart won't be able to sustain you." From the sounds of it, Monica just knew she was going to die at any minute. It was like telling her she had AIDS.

Terrence finally said something, "A medically induced coma!" he still had no idea of what the doctor was talking about, "What is a medically induced coma?" he asked very concerned.

The doctor explained to the both of them what would happen. "I will administer a controlled dose of propofol medication to keep your heart pumping and keep your blood pressure up. We have to protect your brain and parts of the brain that are not getting the blood necessarily…"

All Monica was hearing was gibberish. "How long will I have to be that way?" she questioned looking at her daughter.

"It depends on how serious your problem is. We will run further tests to find the cause. It can be six months, it really depends on, and it depends on your progress of healing. Now, this is solely up to you, this is a decision that you and your husband will have to make. You will need to make a decision soon, Monica, this is a serious matter."

"I want to do whatever is best for me. How soon can you start the process?"

"We can start immediately; you want to start before it's too late."

"Okay, I just will have to make some arrangements, you know, I do have a child and all." She looked over at Terrence. He gave her an assuring look as if he had her.

"Sure, no problem; do you have any more questions for me?"

"I guess," she said sadly. She and Terrence looked at one another.

"The nurse will be in here to check your vitals, and I will begin to put things in motion and make preparations for you. I will take care of you." he then assured her.

"Wow, Monica, respiratory failure..." he shook his head.

Tears rolled down her face. She couldn't believe what she was hearing. *"How is this possible she thought?"* Her last check-up with her physician, she was fine; all labs and test were good.

Terrence walked to her side of the bed, reached in, and gave her a sincere hug with tears in his eyes. "I am so sorry," he whispered in her ear.

She nods her head up and down, not able to say a word. She was stuck; she had lumps in her throat, and just couldn't say anything. She took a deep breath and exhaled. "What about my baby?"

Terrence released his hug and began rubbing her back. "What do you mean, what about her? I'm going to really help you out with her until you get out of here. I will bring her up here to see you every day. You don't have to worry about that. Focus on you getting better and getting the hell outta' here."

She looked up at him, "Terrence, I don't want any problems, I can't take too much. This is enough stress on me," she told him in an exhausted tone.

"You don't have to worry about nothing, I got you."

"Look in that drawer and get my house keys, just in case she needs anything."

"She's good, whatever she need I'll just buy it."

The nurse had come in to give Monica some medication to help ease her pain and discomfort; she dozed off with Aleena in her arms. Once Terrence realized that she was sleeping, he quietly grabbed his daughter and headed to the house.

Chapter 17

"So, how's Monica doing?" Brooklyn asked Terrence.

Aleena laid sleep on the couch next to her dad. "She's not doing too well before I left, the doctor told her she has respiratory failure, and she will be put in a medically induced coma."

"Respiratory failure, what! Oh wow, a medically induced coma. She really must not be doing too good. Damn!" she couldn't believe it. "She's so young." Did Brooklyn really care or was she just faking it? "So, what are you going to do with, she?" she asked, pointing to Aleena, she rubbed her head as if she was concerned.

"She's gonna have to stay here. Where else is she gone go, I am her daddy."

"Yeah, you sure are. I didn't say you weren't."

"Brooklyn, don't start,"

"Don't start what? All I was going to say was I'll help you with her for the time being."

"Oh ok, that's cool." Terrence picked up Aleena, took her, and laid her on the bed.

"You know you might end up having to get legal custody of Aleena while Monica is in that condition. Respiratory failure ain't anything to play with, your system can shut down fast," she told him as he walked back in. She got up went into the kitchen and began to prepare some food.

Terrence sat at the table and put his head in his hands. "This shit here, man. I don't know how to go about that shit." At this point, he was irritated.

"Well, shit, don't get mad at me. I'm trying to help you out." Since he and Monica were married, he didn't really have to do all that, but she didn't want to tell him that, he didn't know she knew they were married and that's how she was going to keep it for now.

"Yeah, well, I'll worry about that later. When I go back up there, I'll talk to her about some things."

"When you go back up there?" she asked as if she wasn't the mother of his child.

"Brooklyn, really, so I'm not supposed to care or even take my daughter up there to see her mother?"

He just touched a nerve with her at that moment. She left the food there she was cooking, turned the fire off, and walked off into the bathroom.

He shook his head, "I'll be back!" he yelled.

"Wait, no you not about to..." by the time she made it out the bathroom and to the door, Terrence was out of there. "... Leave her here with me," He left Aleena there not giving a damn how she felt about it. He wasn't trying to hear shit she was saying. And to keep his hand off her, he just left. *"This motherfucker got his fucking nerves. Now, what in the hell am I going to do with her."* Brooklyn had plans to be with Corey, furthermore, she had to go to work. She didn't have time to be watching no kids.

She called Corey and explained to him that she might not be making it. He told her whenever she gets a chance to come by anyway, no matter what time it is; he had a surprise for her. She told him, okay and she will try her best to come by when she gets off work. "And bring your overnight bag with you too," he told her. Curious to know, she called Brittney and told her everything that was going on. As much as Brittney didn't want to do it, she didn't want her sister missing work, so she told her she will keep Aleena for her until she gets off work. After packing Aleena something, she hurried and took her over to Brittney's place.

***

"Thanks, sis, I really appreciate this," Brooklyn told Brittney while dropping off Aleena.

"Yeah, no problem, anytime, what are sisters for?"

"I owe you big time,"

"Yeah, you do. I'll make sure to remind you."

"Whatever, I'll see you later, girl, thanks again."

"Alright,"

Brooklyn went on to work the whole time thinking about what surprise Corey had for her. This day she had it easy at work. She had an intern working under her, so she put her to work making things easier on herself. Maybe Corey was going to take her out somewhere, she didn't know, she just didn't want to wear herself out.

Before getting off work, she called Corey and told him that she was on her way…

***

When Brooklyn, arrived at Corey's door, she could smell marijuana coming straight through the door. When he let her in, he had music playing low and the lights were dim. "Hey, Mr. what you got going on in here?" she asked, giving him a hug and a kiss.

"I miss you," he told her, rubbing her butt.

"I see, so what's up?" she scanned the area.

"Don't be scared," he said. "Want you hop in the shower," Brooklyn didn't ask any questions. When she walked in the bathroom, the shower water was running and a sexy black lingerie was laid out for her, no panties, next to some fragrance lotion with a note under it that read;

"Don't put this lotion on just the lingerie, and when you are done, come into the room."

After her shower, she walked in the room, candles were lit and it smelled real good in there. She just knew she was going to be relaxed, relaxation was just what she needed.

Corey grabbed the lotion out of her hand and placed a blindfold over her eyes. "Lie across the bed on your stomach, relax and close your eyes." She followed along, still not asking any questions. She loved how he made her feel. She positioned herself across the bed. He rubbed lotion in his hands and began massaging her feet. The massage went from her feet to her butt. She exhaled, feeling a tingle through her body, "Turn over," he told her. She turned over, blindfold still on. Her legs were spread open and she felt soft lips and a tongue tastes her sweetness.

"Mm," she moaned, pussy wet.

The oral pleasure stopped, Corey stood over her head and removed the blindfold.

She blinked her eyes and when she gained focus, she saw a bad female standing in front of her. "Corey," she called.

"Brooklyn this is my friend, Taya,"

Corey brought up threesomes with her before and asked her how she would feel about having one. She never took him seriously and just joked around with him. Now it was really happening. She fantasized about it before, with Terrence of course, because he had even mentioned it to her before. But, she never thought it would really be happening, especially with Corey.

She looked at Taya, Taya stood there naked, her body was banging. She favored Amber Rose, but instead of a blond, bald head, hers was red. She was a sexy, attractive Redbone, and Brooklyn found her to be very attractive. She looked back over to Corey, "Is this what you really want?" she asked. He told her, yeah, and from there she was turned out ever since.

"Come here," he told her. She got up and sat on the edge of the bed. He then gestures for Taya to come over to them. "Do your thing, ma," he told Taya. He sat in a chair he had by the bed, shirt off, boxer briefs on, and was hard like wood.

Taya began kissing Brooklyn and she followed suit. New to this, but it was feeling as if Brooklyn had done it before, everything was coming naturally and she loved every bit of it. Taya wasted no time, laying her back. She licked and kissed softly on Brooklyn nipples. Already experienced, Taya took control and pleased her in every way while Corey watched and recorded. It was feeling so good to Brooklyn; she never even paid any attention to him filming them. After Taya pleased her, they switched positions, now Taya on her back. Brooklyn was in a zone; she licked, sucked, and pleased Taya as if she had done it before. While Brooklyn tasted Taya's juice box, Corey couldn't take watching anymore, he joined in and stood over Taya's face and she engulfed him with pleasure. Corey loved having his cake and eating it too.

When Brooklyn glanced up, Taya was slurping away on Corey's manhood. "Lay down," Taya told him. He laid on his back and was receiving face from both girls, eyes closed and feet curled...

Chapter 18

Before Monica was put in a medically induced coma, she and Terrence arranged for him to keep Aleena, even making him her power of attorney. What she was going through just didn't feel real. Terrence kept his promise and brought Aleena to see her, at least, two times a week. He would have brought her more often, but he couldn't take seeing her hooked up to all those machines. Moreover, Aleena would always cry when she was up there. Of course, she didn't know what was going on, all she knew is, she wanted her mommy, she was missing her.

The doctor told Terrence, that it is good if he talks to her, although she doesn't respond, she can probably hear him. So every time he goes up there, he will talk to her and hold her hand. When Aleena was there, Monica would have reactions to if she knew her baby was present.

Terrence decided to visit Monica and leave Aleena at the house. Brooklyn constantly rang his phone, he never answered. He told her he was going to make a stop to check on the Laundromat and handle some business. He sat in the hospital chair with his feet kicked up, playing on his phone.

Clears throat, "So you don't know how to answer your phone?" Brooklyn walked in the hospital room with Aleena.

Terrence quickly looked up and said, "What the fuck are you doing here?"

"I'm bringing you y'all daughter since you don't know how to answer your phone. Terrence, I am not your built-in babysitter."

Monica's monitors began to go off, "You need to go home and get out of here!" he told her.

"Why in the fuck would you lie and say you were going somewhere else?"

The nurse came into the room. "I'ma need for you guys to step out for a minute."

"You see what the fuck you did?"

"Fuck you, Terrence!" They both walked down the hall and into the waiting area. "Here, take your daughter."

"You need to take your ass home; you have no business up here!"

"You have no business up here your damn self with yo' lying ass! If you are not bringing Aleena up here to see her, you shouldn't even be up here." Brooklyn held back no punches. She had no idea that he was a power of attorney over Monica if she knew she would really flip.

"Give me my daughter, and take your stupid ass home."

"Stupid, I got your stupid, mother fucker."

Terrence nodded his head, "Okay, I got you, I'll be home later." He took his daughter and left out the waiting room, leaving her standing there.

Brooklyn drove home to get ready for work she was pissed. She knew when he got home it would be a problem, so she stayed the night at her sister's house. She would have gone to Corey's, but didn't feel like dealing with him, she needed her sister instead.

***

"I just can't believe him," Brooklyn told Brittney.

"I can,"

"How he gonna keep leaving me with his daughter, the fuck I look like his damn babysitter?"

"Yup, you hit it right on the nose. B, when are you going to wake up? This is getting crazy."

"I know, I know."

"I don't know why you don't want to listen to me, I ain't told you nothing wrong yet. I don't know what's going on with you. I'm starting to think you like him treating you like this, because why would you keep taking his bullshit."

"I'm going to leave him, trust me. I just have to find the right time."

"What?" Brittney didn't know what was going on with her sister and was concerned about her. "Don't wait until it's too late. You need to leave while you can."

"Ah, I need a drink; I can't take this anymore."

"That's exactly why you need to leave before it gets worse than it already is."

"Okay, I hear you; you don't have to keep saying it."

Was Brooklyn going to finally take heed and listen to her sister, or was she going to continue to be unhappy in a relationship that she knew herself wasn't going anywhere?

***

As time passed, Brooklyn, grew to love Aleena as her own. She thought why treat her wrong, she's just a child, she didn't ask for this. While Terrence was out, "taking care of business", she snuck and took Aleena to see Monica.

She walked in the hospital room holding Aleena and stood next to the bed looking at her, look lifeless on a breathing machine.

"Hi, how are you?" a nurse asked as she walked in the room. "Hey little Aleena," the nurses knew her by name because Terrence always brought her up there.

"Hi, I'm good and you? How is she doing?"

"Uh, not too good, we are keeping a close watch on her. Are you family? Haven't seen you up here before,"

"Yes, I'm her cousin. I don't live close by, so I'm not able to come up here much."

"Oh, I see, I understand."

Before the nurse could check her vitals, the monitors began to go off. "Just a minute," she told Brooklyn.

"What's going on, is she okay?"

"I think she can hear us at times. I have noticed when a familiar voice is in the room this tends to happen." The nurse silenced the machines that were going off and continued with her vitals.

Brooklyn sat Aleena down in a chair and rubbed Monica's head. "Don't worry cousin, you will be ok, Aleena is in good hands." The machines went off again. "We'll step out for a minute until you are finished."

"Okay, that will probably be best."

"Yeah, you're right." Instead of stepping out for a minute, Brooklyn just left the hospital. She just wanted to see and hear for herself the progress of Monica's condition. She no longer trusted anything that Terrence told her. From her nursing experience, it seemed as if Monica did know when someone was present.

Chapter 19

Corey found out what Brooklyn was doing. One day he went through her phone and in her notes; she had personal income and account balance information with no name to it with numbers that looked to be a bank account number. He couldn't believe the balance amount he was seeing. He asked her about it and she lied, telling him she was helping a friend out with a money situation she was having with her dad. Then she questioned him about why was he going through her phone. He told her he wanted to see if she was hiding anything, such as talking to other men. She put a passcode on her phone so that nobody would be able to get into it, and then she deleted everything she had in it. After that, he would watch her closely without her knowing.

Terrence would only deposit money here and there and would only draw out money every month for living expenses. Brooklyn kept a close watch on his activities, he was never aware that she added herself as an authorized user on his account; having access to all his coins.

She was cutting it off with Corey because he was a hoe just like Terrence. The only thing that was different with him, he was honest about his doings. She didn't want to share a man with other women. Yeah, she had her fun; however, she wanted her man to herself. Corey wasn't willing to let go of the others, so she was calling it quits. She was going to take all of Terrence's money and skip town, starting a new life. Corey knew if he kept her around, he could get the money, so when she tried to break it off with him, he begged her to stay. The begging, pleading, and trying to convince her to stay just wasn't working, so he flipped the script on her and told her,

"If you don't stay, I will go to the police with what you told me, and I will give Terrence the video of you, me, and Taya."

When Brooklyn found out that Terrence was married to Monica, and also planning to leave her for Monica, she flipped. *"How could he!"* She knew something had to be done to keep them from being together. There was no way Monica was getting a chance at what Brooklyn felt was hers. Although Monica was still alive, it seemed as her spirit was hunting her, she felt she needed to tell somebody, so she confided in Corey and told him that she poisoned her.

When Brooklyn and Monica went out to lunch to make amends, the waiter brought their drinks after Monica got up to go to the restroom. While in the restroom, Brooklyn slipped some Methanol in her drink to get rid of her for good.

Brooklyn couldn't believe what she was hearing from Corey, "You would what? You wouldn't dare,"

"Leave out that door and you will see,"

"Oh, so you a rat now?" she didn't know if he was bluffing or not. She continued on leaving.

"Let that door close, and all that money you have access to will be reported, and you won't get a dime."

Her eyes got big, and she turned around. "All the what?"

"Yeah, you heard me right— All that money you have access to will no longer be in your possession."

"This bitch ass, nigga no his snitch ass didn't. Damn, I just can't find a solid man for shit." she thought to herself.

"If you don't give me half of what you have, I will go to the police and turn you in."

From the look on his face and the sound of his voice, he was very serious. Brooklyn turned around dropped everything and took a seat on the couch. He did a complete 360 on her. Where was this coming from? "How you..."

"Don't worry about how I know," he said, cutting her off, "just know that I know."

"Okay, but, it's not going to be that easy for me just to get half of that money out with nobody being suspicious," she told him, thinking of a plan.

"Well, you got two weeks." He didn't know who money it was and he didn't care, all he knew was that he wanted a piece of it. *But for what, he made good money?* Greed just got the best of him. Everybody always wants a piece of the pie.

She couldn't believe what he was saying to her. She fell for this man gave her all to him, and was being honest with him. *How dare him!* Her heart was just being ripped into little pieces. *"What is it with me and men?"* she would question. *"Two weeks, this motherfucker is out his mind,"* she thought. "Two weeks? Okay, I will do it by then. You bet not try to play me after I give you the money and still go to the police. I need your word."

"You got my word."

After how these men treated her wrong abusing and lying to her, how could she trust him? That was just a chance she had to take. It was either the money or he'd turn her in.

***

Exactly two weeks later, Corey called Brooklyn over expecting her to have the money he was demanding.

This night she had to go to work. Instead of her going in at her regular time, she went in early clocked in and left without anyone seeing her. Clocking in early wasn't' anything unusual for her, she had done it many times. She was a good worker and a great Charge Nurse, she got away with a lot at her job, they needed her. She didn't know what Corey was capable of, and didn't want to take any chances, so she left work to meet him.

As she drove to his house, she was going to call him to let him know that she was on her way, but her phone wasn't getting any service or working right, so she just cut it off. She pulled over to the nearest phone booth and called him. "I am on my way." Before he could respond, she hung up. As she was pulling up, she saw one of his female friends leaving from his house.

When she walked in, he had already been drinking, and offered her a drink, "No thank you, gotta go to work tonight."

"Alright, well more for me. So what's up, did you get it?"

"No, I just need a little more time,"

"A little more time, for what and for how long?"

"Why are you rushing it, it's not going anywhere. I can't just go pulling out money, making things look suspicious. Just please, be patient. You got it coming, trust me."

He was drunk, in a good mood, and feeling himself. "Here, have a drink," he told her pouring her a glass."

"You can sit it down, I'll get it."

Corey's phone went off and he walked into his room to take the call. Brooklyn took out her secret weapon, some Methanol and poured it into his drink. After seeing how it did Monica, she put more in his glass. Before he came out the room, she poured some of her drink out as if she had drunk some of it, and then wiped her glass off.

"So I see you changed your mind," he told her looking at her glass.

"Yeah, I figured a little won't hurt," she got up from the couch. He grabbed her by her arm, pulled her close and kissed her. What was with these men? "Just give me a day or so, okay." She kissed him again.

"Don't be playing, Brooklyn, don't forget I have that tape."

"Trust me, you will have it."

He picked up his glass and took a swig from it. He walked her to the door and told her if she can, come back when she get off work. Her response was, "I'll try." He opened the door for her and let her out.

***

A couple days later,

Brooklyn hadn't heard from Corey, he hadn't called her and she hadn't called him. She had cracked her phone to the point it was inoperable.

"Please, help, send someone now! He's... He's, dead." A female voice cried out on the phone after dialing 911.

"Hello, ma'am, who's dead? What happened? Help is on the way, I'm sending the police now," the 911 operator on the other line stated.

The phone went dead as the operator sat listening to the dial tone. "Ma'am, hello, are you there?"

Nothing…

Taya sat next to Corey on the floor looking at his lifeless body. When she got there he was already about to pass out. She asked him was he okay, but he wasn't able to respond, he barely could breathe. Minutes later, he clasped right in from of her on the floor right where he died.

When the paramedics and police came, he was gone; it was nothing they could do. They questioned Taya, and she told them all she knew. Since she was there at the time of his death, she was considered a suspect; she wasn't under arrest pending further investigation.

Chapter 20

With Monica in the hospital and after Corey's death, Brooklyn didn't think there would be any more problems between her and Terrence, until…

"Hello, Brooklyn," a voice said when she answered the phone.

"Oh, shit, here we go," she thought. "This is Brooklyn. Who's calling?"

"This is Dion. I spoke to you a while back."

"Oh, Dion, yeah, the Dion that called looking for Terrence. Yes…" she paused for a second, "what you want and how in the hell did you get my number, bitch?"

"Look, I don't want any problems. Honestly, I wanted to talk to you about, Terrence…"

Brooklyn interrupted, "What about him, you fucking him too? Well, honey, let me be the first to tell you that you are not the first one."

"If you don't mind, I would want to tell you in person. I can't continue to do this."

Something about this woman was strange; you could hear it all in her voice. What was it? *"This bitch bet not tell me her ass is pregnant."* Brooklyn thought. "In person... how I know this ain't a joke?"

"Because I'm telling you it's not, and it is something you need to know."

"You know what? I don't have time for no bullshit. If you are fucking around, it's going to be a problem."

"We can meet in the open, somewhere public. If you want to know everything, just meet me at Mayfair Park. You can call this number back when you make it up there. I'll be there in about fifteen minutes." Dion told her.

"Alright, I'll see you up there."

When Brooklyn hung up the phone, she phoned Brittney. "Hey, Brit, what you doing?"

"Sitting here folding up this last load of clothes, what's going on?

"Some female name, Dion, called me a minute ago."

"Okay, and who is Dion?"

"I guess she is somebody that Terrence nasty dick ass been fucking. She called his phone before, but didn't say too much. Now she wants to meet up and tell me what's been going on with them."

"So, what, you going to go meet her?"

"Yeah, I'ma meet her; so, if anything happens or you don't hear from me, I will be at Mayfair Park."

"You need me to roll with you?"

"No, I'm good. I was just letting you know where I will be at."

"Ok, I got you. Be safe. Keep your eyes open just in case she tries to pull some funny shit."

"Oh, don't worry, I am. I'll call you later."

"Ok, bye."

"Bye."

Brooklyn hung up the phone and set it on her dresser, put on some jeans, a girl-T, a pair of Samoa Adidas, and headed out the door. Not knowing what to expect, she grabbed her pepper spray, pocket knife, a .22 semi-automatic pistols, her keys, and headed out the door.

***

Once Brooklyn, arrived at the park, she phoned Dion to let her know she was there. Dion told her where she was sitting at and for her to come where she was. Brooklyn saw a brown-skinned woman sitting at a picnic table and walked over to her…

"Are you Dion?" she said when she approached her.

Dion looked up from texting on her phone, "Yeah, I am Dion."

Brooklyn looked her up and down in a weird way. She wasn't cute at all, but she did have a nice shape. A little heavy with the makeup too, but was dressed cute. She had on some fitted jeans a loose fitting blouse that exposed her breast a little. Brooklyn got pissed, however, played it cool when she saw Terrence's name tattooed across her chest. *"Are you serious, what does he see in her?"* she asked herself. "So what's up, what's the deal, why did you want me to come here? Just get right to it."

"Do you want to sit down?" Dion asked her.

"Sit down? Hell no, I want to know what you have to say."

"Well, Terrence and I have been dating for a while now."

"Dating, and what do you mean by dating... Like going out to a movie and dinner type of dating or more intimate dating?"

"We have been intimate. But now he wants to play these games, putting me on hold."

"What do you mean on hold? You knew he had a woman, but you still chose to sleep and fuck with him. Now that's your fault. And you can keep his ass because I'm 'bout done with him anyway. And why you want to come out now and tell me you are fucking my husband?"

"I wanted to tell you, but I was getting paid to keep quiet. But I can no longer continue to be in the closet. I am a transgender; I was born a man..."

"You are a what! Nah, no, uh, uh," Brooklyn was at a loss for words. Her heart was now in her stomach. Tears fell down her face and she immediately ran to the nearest trash can to vomit in it.

Dion walked over there to her, "Brooklyn, I'm sorry you had to find out like this," she told her.

"Get the fuck away from me!" she yelled gagging.

Dion stepped back and went to sit back at the picnic table. *"Oh My God, did I really tell her that? Oh shit, I think I fucked up,"* she thought.

After Brooklyn finished vomiting up her insides, she walked back over to the table. "Tell me that this is a joke and that you are lying?"

"I wish I could, but it's true."

"So, you mean to tell me, my man is fucking a man? Do you have a Vagina? Please, at least, tell me you do."

She stood there shaking her head, "No… no, I don't."

"Oh Lord!" Brooklyn's head was pounding. It was taking everything in her to remain calm and not flip the hell out. "And he knows that you are a man and have a dick between your legs?"

"Yes, he knows all of that."

"Uh, uh, I need proof. How do I know you're not just making this shit up to come between our marriage?" Brooklyn was hoping that this was all a lie. *"No wonder why this bitch was looking weird and sounding all funny."*

"That night you caught him with that stripper at his party, he was with me later that night, that's how I know. I came to pick him up not too long after you left."

She couldn't believe what she was hearing. How do you deal with the fact that your man is sleeping with another man that dresses like a woman? How could she have missed that?

"Here, so that you know that I am not making this up," Dion scrolled through her phone. "See,"

Brooklyn gasped for air covering up her mouth. The tears would not stop flowing. She was looking at a picture of Terrence lying on his back with Dion's penis in his mouth.

"This sick nasty bastard!"

She grabbed the phone and started going through it, looking at pictures of them and text messages between the two. "I can't, I just can't. You can have him, I can't do this. This is the last straw for me." She sat Dion's phone on the table and walked off…

She went to her car and drove off. She turned down a side street and parked her car. "A man, a fucking man?" she put her head down on the steering wheel and just cried her heart out... She called to tell her sister.

Any other time, Brittney would believe something Terrence did with the quickness because he was such a dirty dog, but this, this was something she just couldn't believe. She would have never thought. Now, what was Brooklyn going to do?

Chapter 21

Brooklyn sat at the kitchen table combing Aleena's hair. "You still going by Anthony's?" she asked Terrence as he walked in the kitchen.

"Yeah, I'm about to leave in a minute. Why, what's up?"

"Oh, um, I wanted you to give your auntie her birthday gift for me."

"Yeah, alright,"

"I'll go put it in the car because I don't want you to mess it up, it has to be set a certain way."

"Man, ain't nobody gone mess that shit up."

"Whatever," she stated, getting up grabbing the gift bags from on the side of the couch and took it outside to the car.

"How long it's gone take you to finish her hair. I was gone take her with me to get her out of your hair."

"Oh, no, it's cool. I was going to take her to John's Incredible Pizza, and I already told her."

"Alright, well, here." He pulled two hundred dollars out of his pocket and gave it to her.

Brooklyn proceeded to take the gift bags. When she made it to the car, she placed the bags neatly in the trunk. She slammed the trunk and walked off with a smirk on her face.

"How long are you going to be gone?" she asked.

"I don't know, why what's up?"

"I was just asking, no worries." She continued to comb Aleena hair.

Terrence grabbed his Pepsi out the refrigerator. "Alright, I'll be back later, I'll call you," he told her and then left.

When he walked out the door, she rolled her eyes. *"Ugh, I can't stand him,"* she said to herself. At times, he just disgusted her, just about every little thing he did would irk her. The way he would eat his food, how he would always be on his phone, how he would chew his gum; she just couldn't stand him anymore. He broke her, turned her heart cold. She vowed never to put a man first in her life, but God. Her next relationship if it would be any, she told herself that she would make sure she made herself happy first, before trying to make a man happy. She always pushed to please her man and keep him happy, thinking that it would keep him and just to show him that her love was real and true, not once seeing how it was making her feel; sad, hurt, used, lied to, just ran over. For a while, she didn't even care, doing that, left her with a broken heart and soul. She felt she couldn't love anymore, didn't want to give herself to another and get let down and hurt again. She learned from her mistakes, no more being *Blinded by Love, "Never again,"* she said.

***

Terrence sat in his driver's seat, leaned back, tinted windows rolled up, AC blows, weed smoke in the air, banging, Cayceegee's *'Straight From the Heart'*. He looked down a quick second to check a text message,

Brooklyn: **Terrence, Aleena is cutting up, she is having temper tantrums, I'm unable to control her and don't want to hit her.**

No Good Bastard: **Where y'all at?**

Brooklyn: **Still at the house.**

No Good Bastard: **Damn, all right I'm about to turn around.**

Brooklyn: **No, I have to go to the bank anyway, just meet me on Rosecrans and Van Ness by Church's Chicken, since you are over that way by the Laundromat.**

No Good Bastard: **Damn, All right.**

He made it to the parking lot, parked and waited for Brooklyn to come. About twenty minutes had past. He picked up the blunt that he had put out and lit it back up, and then texted her phone,

No Good Bastard: **Damn, where you at?**

Brooklyn: **I'm coming, it was an accident on the highway, and I had to pull over to calm her down.**

No Good Bastard: **All right, just hurry up!**

When he looked back up, he saw two cop cars behind him with their lights flashing. *"Shit!"* He put the blunt out and stashed it.

All the officers hopped out, guns drawn. Two of the officers approached the window slowly and tapped on it; tap, tap, tap. "Can you roll your window down, sir?"

Chyna S.

Terrence barely cracked his window. "Why, what did I do?" he asked. The other officer walked around to the passenger's side trying to see in the car.

"I'ma need you to roll your window down, whose car is this?"

"What you mean, whose car is this? This my car, why?"

"License and registration,"

"I'm pulling out my wallet," he warned, Terrence took his Driver's license out, passed it to the police, leaned over, took his registration and insurance out the glove compartment, and passed it through the crack of the window.

"Do you have any weapons or drugs in here?"

"No, I don't,"

The officer took the information and walked back to his patrol car to verify it. Terrence rolled his window back. The other officer walked over to the driver's window and tapped on it, can you roll your window down, sir?" Terrence cracked the window. "Are you on parole?"

"No, I'm not," he stated and rolled the window back up.

The officer stood positioned with his gun still drawn. The officer that ran his name walked towards the car, the other cops met him halfway, and they stopped and whispered to each other, looking towards the car.

Terrence watched from the rearview window. *"What the fuck are they doing?"*

The officer walked up to the car and tapped on the window. "Sir, I'ma need for you to step out of the car!" the rookie cop told him.

The window came down, "Step out of my car for what, I didn't do anything. I'm waiting for my wife to meet me here

130

with my daughter." Brooklyn still hasn't made it to him yet. *"Where in the fuck is she at?"*

"You have a warrant and you need to get out the car." Terrence grabbed the door handle, the officer pulled out and pointed his weapon, "Nice and slow, hands where I can see them!" He stepped out the car and was handcuffed and put against their car while being read his rights. "You have the right to remain silent..."

"You have any weapons or drugs in here?" the other police asked.

"I just told yo' ass *no,*" he answered, looking up in the air.

They began searching the car. Everything was clean on the inside. "Clear," one officer said, and then popped the trunk. The officers walked to the trunk to search it.

The officer grabbed his aunt's gift bags, "Be careful with that, that's my aunt's birthday gifts."

"Shut your ass up," he told him. He opened one of the bags, and began taking out and rambling through the tissue paper, "Birthday gifts my ass, whose drugs is this?"

"Drugs! Man, what the fuck you talking about?"

The officer pulled out a brick of cocaine followed by another one, and then three pictures. "This is what the fuck I'm talking about." They looked in the other bag and it was two more in there with two pictures. "Looks like someone's gonna be gone for a while." He and the other officer looked through the pictures; they looked at him, and then back at the pictures.

"That shit ain't mine! Those are not my drugs!" he stressed. *"That fucking bitch! I know she didn't!"* he said to himself, shaking his head.

"Yeah, yeah, tell that to a Judge, but as of now, buddy, you're going to jail. You're going to fit right in where you are going." Sargent Ford told him, putting the pictures in his face.

Terrence's eyes got big, *"What the fuck!"* it was pictures of him and Dion, sexually explicit pictures, pictures of him and Dion both with each other's penis in their mouth. A picture of Terence with Dion bent over hitting him from the back, no condom. Terrence was speechless... "Get that shit out my face!"

They removed the pictures, put them back in the bags with the drugs, called a tow to come pick up the car, and put Terrence in the back of the squad car.

Terrence didn't know what was going on, he was shocked at it all. He began thinking, *"She said she was putting my aunt's gifts in the trunk. That sneaky snake ass bitch, this bitch set me up! Nah, nah, man!"* he couldn't believe it.

***

While one day on her way to see Corey, Brooklyn got pulled over by a cop, a Sargent. He was about six feet tall, dark chocolate, bald head sexy thing. Can you say *chocolate drop*; this man was sexy as hell, and don't think he didn't think she was fine, that was an understatement, he had told her, she was the baddest woman he had ever seen, badder than his wife. He never found black women attractive, but seeing Brooklyn changed his mind. His wife was white; he never even dated a black woman. By the sound of his voice, you can tell he was somewhat whitewashed. But he was still fine as hell.

He explained to her why he was pulling her over, because of a broken tail light. She told him seriously, "Officer, I'm sorry, I have a broken tail light? I didn't know."

She got out that ticket, he didn't write her one, instead, he wrote his name and number on a piece of paper and told her, "Take this and call me, I would love to take you out."

No ticket, no nothing, plus he was sexy as hell. Corey or Terrence didn't have anything on this man. She took his number, smiled, and said "Oh, sure, and thanks. I'll give you a call this week."

"Make sure you get that light checked out, and you have yourself a good day," he told her with a smile. His smile alone had sexy all on it. She could have taken him down right there.

"Okay, I will, thanks again, Sargent Ford."

"You can call me, Brandon."

"Will do," She rolled up her window, started her car, slid his number in her purse, and drove off.

After that, someway, somehow, she made ways to see him, going out on dates from time to time. She had told him she was single. She never let him in her personal life. Having an officer, a Sargent as a friend was a plus for her. She tipped him off and told him when and where Terrence was going to be. She could care less about Terrence and what he was going through; he didn't give a damn about her and her heart, so why should she. He brought her to this point of no return!

After he was arrested, Terrence called multiple times collect trying to get through to Brooklyn, but was unsuccessful. Finally, after being locked up for some weeks, she answers her phone and put money on it for the call to go through.

"What's up with you, B? Why you haven't been answering my calls?"

"I didn't have money to put on the phone."

"Man, stop fucking playing, you set me up. How could you do some shit like that?"

"Set you up, what are you talking about, Terrence. Why would I set you up?"

"Yeah, play dumb if you want. How in the fuck did dope get in those gift bags that *you* put in my trunk?"

"Look, Terrence, I have no idea of what you are talking about. Maybe, Dion put them in there because you weren't trying to give *him*, I mean *her* no more dick!"

He got quiet, "Brook, baby, I can explain."

"Explain what? I don't need your gay ass trying to explain to me why you were fucking a tranny. You got me all the way fucked up; I'm done with your taking dick in the ass bullshit. You might find you a nice one in there bitch!" she hung the phone up in his face.

He tried to call her back and she didn't answer. Brooklyn packed all of her and Aleena's things. She had paid a good friend that worked at Bank of America to add her name to Terrence's account. She told the bank that they were moving out of town, and buying a house, so she needed to withdraw everything. After she withdrew everything, she closed the account. She told Brittney everything that had happened and what was going on, that she was moving to Atlanta, and if she wanted to go. Of course, Brittney said yes. Her head was hurting from all the things Brooklyn was pouring on her. She couldn't believe she was going through all of that by herself. She wished she had told her, so she could have helped her sister.

The next time Brooklyn talked to Sargent Ford, she was in Atlanta living in a nice five-bedroom, four bath house with a big backyard that had a swimming pool. It looked like a mini mansion. She had adopted Aleena and told him she moved out there to help her grandma and that she adopted her cousin whose mother was on drugs. She later told him her grandmother had passed. He took a flight out there to see her; they started and kept a long distance relationship.

When she moved, Monica was still in a medically induced coma, she took Aleena to see her a few times, and she later passed away.

R.I.P

Michael Wandick

And

Michelle Boykins

You will forever be loved and missed!

ACKNOWLEDGEMENTS

First, I want to give Praise, Honor, Thanks to my most high, The Almighty, my Lord, and Savior, for Blessing me with the talent and strength to write and publish this book, all of my books; He made this possible, and I am so grateful for that. I truly thank you, God, for Blessing me with these two amazing, talented creative hands and brain.

Thank you, husband, for always having my back and believing in me. You are the best husband ever!

To my kids, MuMu, Diddy, O, Lamont, ManMan, and Lamondre, I love all of yall with all I got! You guys keep me going.

Special Thanks to KD Jones and Myi Jenks, for coming through when I needed y'all to read my final work and giving me the green light, I really appreciate it! Love y'all.

I want to thank all who have supported me, I love y'all and I really appreciate it.

Blinded By Love

Blinded by Love, some call it a fatal attraction,
Whenever I'm around you, my heart skips a beat and loose
traction,
Blinded by Love, when I'm not around you I feel all alone;
My heart and soul feel broken until you call and come
home,
Blinded by Love, when it comes down to you its black and
white,
I go hard for your love and will always put up a fight,
Blinded by Love, you are all that I want and all that I have,
In the beginning, you use to hold me, kiss me, and always
make me laugh,
Blinded by Love, you had me wrapped around your finger,
trapped in a daze,
Sometimes feeling claustrophobic, at times wanting to
leave, but couldn't, because I was trapped in your maze,
Blinded by Love, I sacrificed everything, my heart, and
soul just to make you happy,
I took to you fast, because the absence of my daddy,
Blinded by Love, had I had known not to choose so fast;
I would have saved my heart, knew better, and maybe it
would have last,
Blinded by Love, you live and you learn;
I have learned from my mistakes and will let them burn,
Blinded by Love

ABOUT THE AUTHOR

Chyna Sallier established October 19, 1979. Born and raised in Compton, California, and proud to be a Libra. She is the CEO of Queen C's Publishing and the Publisher/Author of her three books titled, Blinded By Love, Hood Girlz 1 and 2. Chyna is also the proud owner and Editor-in-Chief of DIME DIVAAZ magazine. She is also the creator and writer of her up and coming play, Blinded By Love.

Chyna is a smart and talented woman; a high school graduate and is currently enrolled in school, working towards her Bachelors in Business Entertainment. As a teenager, Chyna discovered her God gifted talent in writing; it started from her writing her feelings on notepads, which led to writing stories and poems. Now she is writing and publishing books, magazines, and plays. She is creating real urban / erotic street novels, short stories, and poems. She has no intentions of stopping. Her love for Literature has driven her to persevere through life's challenges and meet her goals of writing and publishing a multitude of artistic expressions. After being in the literacy industry, Chyna has met other wonderful, talented authors and writers that she is working with on other projects. As a devoted wife, loving mother, nurse, author, editor, publisher, entrepreneur, student, and hairstylist, she manages to wear all hats successfully. Chyna is a strong black woman that loves to empower and encourage women through her positive influences. She is a role model for our youth living the lifestyles that she writes about, she encourages youth in the hood not to settle for less. One of her philosophies is that; "Even though you go through struggles in life, don't give up; push to be your best in anything you put your mind to."

www.ingramcontent.com/pod-product-compliance
Lightning Source LLC
Chambersburg PA
CBHW050410030726
47503CB00006B/2115